A Love He Can TRUST

BY

LaVerne St.George

Pittsburgh Connections

~ BOOK ONE ~

Put a little Romance in your life !

LaVerne St. George

This book was originally published in a slightly altered form as a hardcover from Avalon Books, Thomas Bouregy and Company Inc. in 1990, and again in paperback from iUniverse in 2003, under the title *A Private Proposal*. It has been revised and updated.

Open Book Romances
  ~an imprint of Open Book Communications
ISBN 978-0-9891344-7-7
Copyright © 2015 Open Book Communications

Cover Design and Interior format by The Killion Group
http://thekilliongroupinc.com

To George,

A Romantic of the Dark, Quiet and Handsome Kind

CHAPTER 1

The stack of file folders slapped to the floor. Hayley Lancaster sneezed into the rising cloud of dust then groped for a tissue in the pocket of her jeans. Another sneeze shook her, jarring her knees against the floor. The spasm over, she glared at the room's contents. The folders might contain direct mail letters and brochures of prime importance to Mr. David Mansfield, president of Mansfield Inc., but right now they were dusty nuisances.

Hayley slumped back on her heels and surveyed her progress. One file cabinet, its drawers now properly marked, stood along the wall beside its five companions, gleaming black and awaiting Hayley's attention. The contents of several cartons dotted the faded linoleum, each manila folder labeled in neat printing.

"Three hours, and I've filled one cabinet and covered the floor," she grumbled.

For being on the job only two weeks, Hayley wasn't expecting a lot, but two years in library school should have prepared her for more than sorting and filing in a filthy storeroom. *Challenging work.* That phrase in the *Pittsburgh Post-Gazette* ad had captured her imagination. The interview had gone well, and the salary offer had been generous. Challenging work, indeed!

Hayley stretched her arms overhead. Daydreaming was not contributing to her progress. She tucked a stray curl of honey-colored hair under her bandanna and dug another handful of brochures from an open box. Muttering to herself, she concentrated on placing the literature in the correct piles.

"Charity pitch, here. Work-from-home campaign, over there…"

"What are you doing?" a voice thundered from the doorway.

Hayley jumped. The brochures in her hand scattered across the floor, destroying the sorting system. Appalled at the damage, Hayley swung around to face the person in the doorway.

"Just what do you mean by scaring me like that?" Indignant, Hayley straightened her shoulders and brought her hands to her hips. "It took three hours of dust and sweat to get these sorted, and you've made a perfect mess of it!" Even as Hayley fumed, she reacted with sudden alertness. A chestnut-brown, pin-striped suit stood in her line of vision.

The voice ignored her tirade. "I'll ask you again. What are you doing? Are you from the janitor service?"

Hayley's hand shot to the bandanna as her eyes flew to his face. Her arms began to tingle. Not only was the suit impeccable, so was the man. The autumn colors in his clothing complemented his golden coloring and red-brown hair. His expression, now hard and demanding, threw lines across his forehead and around his mouth, setting off the strong bones of his cheek and jaw.

Taking a deep breath to steady herself under his piercing gaze, Hayley crossed her arms. "No, I work here," she said. "Is that all right with you?"

At the obvious sarcasm, the man's eyes widened, revealing their rich blue color. *Like a mountain lake*, Hayley thought as she mentally chalked up a score. But as that blue gaze continued to bear down on her, she wondered who would ultimately win this confrontation. Determined not to give ground, she matched his stare.

Little by little, his perusal changed from demand to curiosity. His eyes left her face and roved leisurely over her shoulders and waist to her thighs. Heat rose in Hayley's cheeks as she remembered how she looked — hair hidden under a red-and-white bandanna, grubby jeans, and a T-shirt that proclaimed she was the property of the University of Pittsburgh.

"Sure," he finally answered. "Fine with me." He renewed his study of her face. "I haven't seen you before. Who do you work for?"

In an instant, Hayley remembered her supervisor's advice: *"Don't take a strange face for granted around here. Our contracts sometimes demand high security. If you don't know someone, ask."*

Silently acknowledging that he might be following company guidelines, yet still annoyed with him, Hayley said bluntly, "I could ask the same of you."

The man's frown softened into a grin. "True, but I asked first."

Hayley's stomach flipped. The grin transformed him from an adult of probably close to thirty to a four-year-old. Hayley conceded defeat and returned the grin. "I'm the new information specialist, Hayley Lancaster." She rose and held out her hand. "I work for Maggie."

"Very glad to meet you, Hayley Lancaster."

From her more advantageous position, Hayley still had to look up to meet his eyes. That fact came as a pleasant surprise since her own height usually dictated a more direct gaze with men. The hand she took engulfed hers in warmth and smoothness. The tingle in her arms slid down her back. To regain control, Hayley withdrew her hand. "And you are…?"

"Oh, yes. Of course. Me." He brushed his jacket aside and slipped his hands into his pants pockets. His smile faded for an instant then grew along with the gleam in his eyes. "My name's Joshua. I work upstairs in accounting." He looked around the cramped room with its row of file cabinets and mountains of boxes. "So you're trying to straighten out this chaos."

Hayley nodded. "An assignment from Maggie. If I had known what I was in for, I would have declined — politely, but firmly." She shrugged. "The bottom line is that Mr. Mansfield is eager to get this done. Anything for the president, I always say, even if it is the most boring job in the company."

Joshua coughed loudly. "Sorry, the dust," he managed in reply to Hayley's concerned glance. Then he continued. "The boss can be… compulsive about things. You wanted something more exciting?"

"I thought I was going to be in the middle of the information field. Developing library services, maybe helping with project proposals." She spread her hands and looked around. "I'm in the middle all right — in the middle of two thousand pieces of paper."

Joshua met her smile with a deep chuckle. Watching his glowing face, Hayley felt a sweep of pleasure. The world tilted just a little.

Joshua brought the chuckle under control, but the humor lingered on his lips. "I see what you mean. But the only thing that can be said for this company is that things always change. Enjoy the boredom. Later you'll wonder where it went."

"I sincerely hope so," Hayley said with feeling. "For now, this is my lot." She looked around, forgetting the man's presence for a moment as she judged what to do next. Suddenly she felt the warmth of his regard and lifted her eyes in question.

"The boss does not approve of blue jeans in the office," Joshua commented lightly.

"Oh, I know," Hayley said, smoothing her jeans in a burst of nervousness. "Maggie told me what a stickler he is for appearances. 'Image is everything in this business.'" Hayley mimicked Maggie's version of the president with a deep voice and a finger pointing in the air for emphasis. "She said it would be all right today because I was working in here."

Joshua's eyes sparkled at her acting. "I thought I'd warn you. Other than playing cleaning lady, are you in the library most of the time?"

An embarrassed flush stole over Hayley's cheeks again, but she managed a faint smile. "Yes, most of the time."

"Then I'll see you later. Perhaps for lunch."

"That would be nice."

"Welcome aboard, Hayley," he said and left.

Hayley rubbed her now-damp palms against her blue jeans. *Why do I always look like something the cat dragged in when I meet a good-looking guy? Three-piece suit meets jeans and T-shirt. Next time I see him, I'm going to be* dressed.

Still, the memory of his appreciative glances convinced her that all was not lost. Humming with newfound gaiety, Hayley shuffled more paper into file folders, raised more dust, and resorted regularly to a box of tissues. One more file drawer was filled when she next glanced at her watch.

"Lunch time and not a moment too soon," she said, sighing. She left everything where it was and closed the door behind her.

Outside in the fluorescent brightness and bustle of the hall, Hayley paused to let a delivery man roll a hand truck piled with boxes toward the elevator. She considered riding up one floor to the accounting department, but her stomach chose that moment to growl.

I'll find out about him later, she thought and turned toward the library.

As she walked, Hayley passed the word-processing room with its bank of desktop computers and network printers. Through the wall of glass, she waved to Kim Mason, one of the dozen word-processing specialists manipulating text for a new directory of musical instruments published by Balsam Press. Balsam was just one of several clients, Hayley knew, who relied on Mansfield Inc. to prepare text for new publications. On her right was the graphics department. Through the windows she could see both artists peering at oversized monitors while their drawing boards waited in readiness.

Her thoughts turned to Joshua, and she mentally reviewed the names of the people she had met in accounting. He wasn't among them. *I wonder when he goes to lunch?* Like a hamster wheel, Hayley's mind spun around and around, pondering her encounter with Joshua. He hadn't touched her, but his gaze had held a caress. No man should be allowed eyes like that! Anyway, she chided herself, a girl shouldn't be so single-minded about a man she'd just met.

Hayley pushed through the glass double doors at the end of the corridor to enter the large room dedicated to collecting and retrieving information on computer and systems technology and the business world. Toward the rear of the library, Hayley could see a staff member at one of the computer terminals that stood beside the more traditional bookshelves and filing cabinets. Casual wood furniture upholstered in shades of blue dotted a corner to her left, inviting the staff to read the latest technology journals. Two offices walled in glass lay to her right. Hayley looked past her office to the second one, where Maggie sat hunched over her terminal, intent on the screen.

Even at the interview, Hayley had liked Margaret Davies' straightforward style, which was reflected in her work and her wardrobe. Tailored suits in bold colors and geometric designs set off Maggie's slim figure. Black hair cut at sharp angles framed a face notable for its straight nose and dark eyes. Next to Maggie, Hayley felt much younger than her twenty-four years — too fair and underdressed. However, within half an hour of that first meeting, Hayley had known she could spend forty hours a week with this woman and be challenged, encouraged, and befriended in the best sense.

As Hayley entered Maggie's office, her supervisor held up her hand for silence, punched one button then another, and leaned back, arms crossed. Shaking her head slowly, Maggie said, "Fifty references and not one of them what I want. I just can't find the right combination. Come take a look."

Hayley rounded the desk and leaned over Maggie's shoulder to scan the titles of the journal articles appearing on the monitor. She had learned the mechanics of database searching in library school. *Choose a topic, translate the concepts into phrases and commands the computer can understand, and poof! A list of articles on the chosen subject.* A few days with Maggie had taught Hayley she had a lot to learn about searching in the real world.

As if reading her thoughts, Maggie said, "This search would be a good one for you to practice on. I could use a second opinion. I'm getting nowhere."

"Any time you say," Hayley said, a touch of anticipation settling in her stomach.

Maggie typed a few commands on the terminal to save her work then swung around in the chair. "How did you do in the closet?"

Hayley smiled. "Not bad. I've separated two boxes of papers, mostly letters from old direct mail campaigns like you thought, and I straightened out the cabinets. I'd like you to take a look at the organization. You may have some other ideas."

"All right." Maggie stood and gathered her papers and printout from the table. "As soon as I can see some daylight in this Alcoa search request. Which will be soon, I hope and pray. Oh, by the way," Maggie said as she filed the papers in her cabinet, "Louise called and said she can't meet you for lunch. The boss is back, and she's deluged."

"You did say he's been gone for three weeks. There's probably a lot backed up." Then Hayley remembered the accountant she had met and asked Maggie about him.

Maggie rested her elbows on the open drawer as she thought. "Joshua? Any last name?"

Hayley pursed her lips then said, "No, he didn't mention it. Come to think of it, he was a little vague about everything." She grinned. "Actually *I* was a little vague about everything. I hardly noticed what he said."

Maggie's eyes twinkled. "That good, huh? I'm sure I would have remembered him, then. Sorry, the name doesn't sound familiar. David does use temporary accountants, especially now, at tax time."

"Temporary?" Hayley shook her head. "He acted like he owned the place."

Maggie laughed. "We'll meet him sooner or later when he needs more information for the IRS All the company records are here." She considered the wall clock a moment then turned back to Hayley. "Just to be safe, call Randy after lunch."

"The personnel director?"

"Right. He hires the temps."

"OK, I'll do that." Hayley checked her watch. "Are you going to lunch?"

The file cabinet shut with a bang. "No, I can't. There's too much to do. Where are you going?"

"Atlantis, I guess."

"Great. Bring me back a gyros with lots of sauce."

"Sure." A bill appeared in Maggie's hand. Hayley took it and said good-bye, but Maggie's attention was already on the papers on her desk.

So the boss is back, Hayley thought as she walked to her office. *Louise will be climbing the walls.*

While she collected her purse and sweater, Hayley chuckled at the image of Louise Whitney literally climbing walls. Her plump figure moved easily enough through company administration, but Hayley doubted it would be up to scaling physical obstacles. Louise wore her brown hair short and neat and dressed with understated taste that fit well with her position as administrative assistant to the president. Louise had once joked with her about what that title encompassed — personal secretary, mother confessor, travel agent, manager of the temp staff, and security guard. No doubt, without Louise and her firm hand, the company would never have reached its one-and-a-half-million-dollar-profit status so quickly.

Hayley and Louise had been to lunch several times, but Louise had warned, *"This won't last. Once David gets back, neither of us will have time to breathe."*

During one lunch, Louise had taken some time to describe the company's activities. Hayley had listened in awe. Mansfield Inc. occupied two floors of one of the new high-rise office buildings that sprang from the steady growth Pittsburgh had been enjoying. On those two floors, ten projects pushed the staff to its limits. For one contract, the staff arranged conferences on new business software for the city. Another contract required the storage and reproduction of solar energy documents as part of an information clearinghouse on alternative energy sources. Several contracts were like the Balsam Press job.

To bring in new jobs, the company wrote at least three proposals a month. With the chance of winning new work running at about one-in-ten tries, proposal writing was an important component of the business.

"With all that goes on here," Hayley had commented, *"David Mansfield must be running at full speed."*

Louise had readily agreed. *"He drives himself too hard and usually expects everyone around him to do the same."* When she had noted Hayley's grimace, Louise had quickly added, *"The other side of the coin is that David cares about the staff. If we've worked overtime to get out a proposal, we can take time off later when the work has slowed. He visits employees in the hospital. He sent flowers to Amy in word processing when she pulled the Dravo disaster out of the water, plus he gave her a raise. A lot of people in this company would throw themselves into the Monongahela River before they'd disappoint the boss."*

And now the boss was back. Standing in front of the elevator, Hayley tried to contain her anxiety at the prospect of meeting a man who seemed to have gained unprecedented staff loyalty. Mentally she shook herself. There was no reason to be nervous. Maggie had said that he would want to meet her when he got back, but with all the work that must be waiting after his vacation, that meeting certainly wouldn't take place for several days. A picture of Joshua as he stood in the doorway of the storeroom flashed through her memory, and she hugged her purse a little closer. *Now if the boss looked half as good...*

The elevator whisked open, and Hayley focused her attention on squeezing into the crowded car and surviving the ride down nine floors while bodies pressed against her on all sides.

She stepped from one crowd into another on the sidewalk and was jostled like a bobbing buoy in high seas until she merged with the flow of pedestrians. Hayley looked up to judge the spring weather. The sky was blue, and one puffy cloud raced across the narrow gap between two tall buildings. Even though she could not see them, Hayley knew that the Ohio, Allegheny, and "Mon" Rivers that flowed through Pittsburgh were sparkling in the sun. Contentment washed over her. On a day like this when the city vibrated around her, Hayley gave thanks for her fortunate move from her smaller hometown to the north and for the job she had found.

A few steps away, Hayley saw the greasy windows with the word *Atlantis* painted across them in fluid script. When she entered, the door banged into a bell. Hayley hardly heard the jangling. The tiny restaurant pulsed with noise: laughing and talking from booths along one wall, the slap of the refrigerator doors sliding shut, and the sizzle of the grill in the back corner.

After shouting her order over one of the glass cases, Hayley watched in amazement as the elderly Greek short-order cook slathered cream cheese onto a bagel, slid the bagel into the microwave, and moved to slice lamb for the gyros, all the while directing his younger assistants in a flurry of Greek.

Hayley smiled. She loved this city with its ethnic cultures, bustling industry, and beautiful parks. Pittsburgh had something for everyone — a world-class symphony, the Carnegie Museum, and the Steelers. The mountains and three rivers added a special touch.

Order now in hand, Hayley made her way back to work and delivered Maggie's sandwich. In her own office, she let down the venetian blinds to cover the windowed walls. The room barely fit a desk, a file cabinet and a coat rack, but Maggie had insisted that everyone needed some privacy, and had cleared this room for Hayley. Pulling down the blinds let everyone know that the occupant was not to be disturbed unless the building was burning or the president called. Hayley blessed Maggie's foresight. After the crowds in the street, a lunch in solitude was what she needed. She was just swallowing the last of the bagel and licking her fingers when a knock sounded, and Maggie walked in.

"There's been a change of plan for this afternoon," Maggie said with a bluntness that reflected the importance of the message. "The boss just called. He has a new RFP that he's all hot about, and he asked if I would send you."

"Me?" The cream cheese stuck in Hayley's throat, and she took a swig from a bottle of cream soda to get it down.

"He wants to meet you and break you into proposal writing."

Hayley swallowed. RFP meant *request for proposal,* a formal query to all interested companies who wanted to bid on a contract.

Other than that, she had no idea how to approach a proposal and said so.

"You'll learn by diving in headfirst," Maggie said.

Hayley's eyes widened in surprise at Maggie's brusqueness.

Maggie shrugged. "You'll do fine. Get a notebook and get up to his office."

Joshua's final words about the boss's dress code rang in Hayley's head. She tugged at her T-shirt. "I can't go like this."

"I'd send you in a paper bag. When the boss says now, he means *now*." With a flick of her skirt, Maggie left.

Hayley took a deep breath. *Something's got her riled*, she thought, then flung open the desk drawer and found her hand mirror. She whipped off the bandanna and ran a comb through her hair, which, she noticed, really needed a trim. The blond curls were more than a little unruly and too long. Her makeup was still in place, but her eyes had widened and darkened to a chocolate brown, a sure sign of nervousness. With a tissue, she wiped her hands and removed a smudge of dust from her cheek. Checking the result in the mirror, she stuck out her tongue at the freckles dusted across her nose. Freckles were so… unprofessional. There was nothing she could do with her clothes, so she found a notebook and walked to the tenth floor.

I wonder what he'll be like? she thought as she ascended the stairs. *If the staff is any judge, he should be nominated for sainthood. And how does an employee relate to a saint?*

With nervous flickers in her stomach, Hayley approached the office door bearing the gold-plated sign that read *Mansfield Inc.* She could hardly breathe, and she stopped outside the door.

"Come on, Hayley, pull yourself together," she admonished herself aloud and squared her shoulders.

When she had visited the reception area to meet Louise for lunch, Hayley had found that the elegant gold and brown decor had relaxed her. Today, Hayley saw only the door in front of her; knowing that David Mansfield awaited her inside made her more than a little anxious.

Louise greeted her from behind the oak desk on the right and smiled in encouragement. "I'll tell him you're here."

Not knowing what to do, Hayley sat down in one of the upholstered armchairs.

Louise leaned into the door of the president's office and said, "Hayley's here."

A familiar, impatient voice sounded from the inner office. "Well, send her in."

CHAPTER 2

Hayley froze. She could not mistake the voice. If she stood among the din of an excited theater crowd on opening night, she would recognize the deep, authoritative tones.

Driven by disbelief and more than a little dismay, Hayley burst off the chair. She brushed past Louise and stopped abruptly inside the doorway. Behind the ultramodern teak desk, wearing the brown pin-stripe suit and, now, a pair of gold wire-rimmed glasses, sat Joshua.

"It's you!" Hayley said. Her amazement threw the words at him with explosive force.

David Mansfield's eyes rose to meet hers, amusement sparkling from behind the glasses. "So it is."

Hayley's shock melted into something near fear. She had not been exactly complimentary to the boss when they had met. On the other hand, she reasoned, he had let her talk. He had given her enough rope to hang herself. Irritation replaced her fear. "Do you always introduce yourself to new employees using a false name?" she demanded.

"False? On the contrary." He tapped the nameplate on the desk with the end of his pen. "J. David Mansfield," he said. "Joshua David. I may not like to use my first name, but it is mine."

Hayley clenched her fists. She detested being the butt of jokes. She didn't even like surprise parties. Though an inner voice warned her to tread carefully, Hayley's pride muzzled the warning. "It was a lousy thing to do. Why didn't you just tell me who you were?"

"And miss that conversation? No, I couldn't resist." At her continued frown, he sighed, removed his glasses, and placed them on the blotter. In the same smooth movement, he rose and walked around the desk, ultimately leaning back on the edge, arms crossed, regarding her with a lopsided grin. "There are ninety people in this company. Everyone knows everyone else, and everyone knows *the boss.*" He enclosed the last words in finger quotes. "It was refreshing to talk to someone who had no idea I was head of this august firm. Have a seat." He motioned to a chrome-and-leather chair and moved to his former position behind the desk. "I have a lot to tell you."

Hayley made no move to obey him. Her mind continued to replay that first conversation. He had made a fool of her.

David reached the other side of the desk and glanced again at Hayley. He slid his hands in his pockets and turned away to study the glittering Pittsburgh skyline. When he faced her, the amusement was gone. "Perhaps I took unfair advantage of the situation…"

"Perhaps?" burst from Hayley.

He held up his hand. "All right, I did take advantage of the situation. But when you didn't know who I was, you were blazingly honest." He watched as Hayley flushed. "Right now, you're thinking of everything you said, trying to remember if you stuck your foot in your mouth to the ankle or all the way up to the knee." He nodded as she blushed even deeper. "I knew it. Believe me, you did neither. You impressed me as a person who can put people and events in perspective. That's good for me and good for the company. The honesty you gave me then I will expect from you in the future."

Hayley felt her irritation fade away to be replaced with wariness. Was he a man who paid only lip service to honesty? Would the rules change in time?

"I'll try," she said.

His eyes still locked to hers, Mansfield said, "That's all I can ask." He sat back into the leather armchair and cocked his head to one side. "I'm glad you took off the bandanna. We do have an image to maintain."

Hayley's eyes flew wide open. She couldn't be sure if he had just paid her a compliment or was crass enough to comment on her clothing again. Her body tensed.

Before Hayley realized he had moved, David was out of the chair and standing in front of her. "I *am* sorry. I've embarrassed you." He touched her elbow and motioned to the chair. "Please."

The soft word coupled with his touch overwhelmed Hayley. She felt like a nervous fawn who had just been given a reassuring nudge from her mother. Hayley raised her eyes and encountered a gaze that reinforced the feeling.

The spell broke as Mansfield backed away from Hayley, confusion and a question clouding his eyes. Abruptly he walked behind the desk, slipped his glasses on, and began shuffling papers.

His movement away from her had changed David Mansfield, the man, to David Mansfield, the president. *Get control of yourself*, Hayley thought. *This is the president of the company, and you're gawking like a teenager. He's so disgusted with you he can't stand to watch your performance.* It was easier for her to believe that than to believe that he might be feeling the same attraction she was attempting to ignore. She moved to the chair he had indicated and sat, opening her notebook efficiently. "What can you tell me about the RFP?" Hayley asked.

David glanced at her. With visible relief, he sat and gathered the pertinent documents in front of him. When he turned his attention to her, he was in control of his voice and his hands.

"It's from the Pennsylvania Department of Environmental Protection, DEP, for short. DEP wants to create a new database of published journal articles and website links that cover how human activity, like manufacturing and mining, affects the environment. The first database they're requesting will cover coal mining, abandoned mines, reclamation, accidents. They consider this a *proof of concept* project. Basically, try it out before expanding to other subjects. The operation will be set up under the direction of the DEP's Southwest Regional Office in Pittsburgh. DEP wants to contract the entire project out and base it downtown. I'll give you this copy of the draft RFP they've released, but I'll go through it with you first and highlight the salient points."

David began a concise description of the requested services. At first, he spoke with businesslike efficiency, but as he explained how Mansfield Inc. might fulfill the terms of the contract, he leaned forward in the chair as if eager to be off. When he made a particularly positive point, he expounded like a college professor determined to engage his young class.

Hayley's interest was sparked of its own volition, matching David's obvious enthusiasm. She forced herself to listen to what he was saying, and she was captivated by the ideas he had for this contract. Her mind now fully occupied, Hayley reviewed the lessons she had learned at school, fitting ideas of her own into David's general scheme. This was what she had studied for — the chance to build something from the ground up. She could plan this online service. She knew it. She had a lot to learn, but what fun it would be to learn, especially with David Mansfield as the teacher.

That unbidden thought whipped her out of the daydream. To her chagrin, Hayley realized that David had stopped and was studying her, waiting.

"I'm sorry, did you ask something?" Hayley said.

A smile tugged at his lips. "Were you thinking about the project or the spring weather?"

"The project," she answered with a catch in her voice. "I was hoping I might be able to suggest some of my own ideas."

"That's just what I was asking. I want you to take your thoughts and the RFP specs and outline a full startup operation. Then talk with the people on this list and put together a rough estimation of manpower, equipment, and computer resources for the project. That will mean an explanation of each task to be performed and the necessary people and materials. In short, what will it take to do this, and does the company have the resources? Can you do that?"

Hayley bit her bottom lip. That honesty he admired reminded her of her inexperience and the enormity of the task he was asking her to undertake. She was eager, but eagerness would not produce a comprehensive project outline. "I've never worked on anything like this before," she admitted.

"Thank you for being honest." His eyes studied her with an innocent expression. "You did say you were bored, didn't you?"

Color rose in Hayley's face. "Yes, I guess I did."

"I do realize you'll need some help. Maggie can give you previous proposals to read." He handed the list of names to her. "Jeff Bauer would be good for the computer work, and Eileen Kaufmann—" he smirked and added, "—*she's* our accountant — can give you the financial background."

Hayley focused her attention on the paper in front of her while her mind whirled. His references to that first meeting drove her crazy. What must he think of her?

"Hayley?"

She had never heard her name quite like that before. The two syllables drifted into the air like a sweet spring breeze.

"Yes?" She looked up to find that he had folded his hands on the desk, his eyes sending her a compelling message.

"This is very important to the company... and to me. You'll soon realize that this project does not involve a lot of money, but if we win the bidding and do a good job, we can have this contract indefinitely. It would stabilize our income and give us a chance to expand the operation."

Hayley's heart skipped. She was conscious of catching what Louise had called the *company epidemic*. At any cost, this man must not be disappointed. Uncertainty washing over her, Hayley said, "Wouldn't you feel more confident with Maggie on this?"

"Maggie has plenty to do." David leaned back in the chair. "Give it a try. You can come to me any time with questions or problems. I'll see what I can do to smooth the way."

Hayley swallowed. The pressure of his confidence did not entirely win her over. But she was not a coward. "When do you want this report?"

"Friday afternoon."

Her breath flew down her throat, and she coughed once then nodded. "I'll try my best, Mr. Mansfield."

David rose and walked around the desk to drape one leg over the corner. "We're going to be working very closely on this, and I like to run an informal proposal writing. Call me David."

This was the last thing Hayley wanted. Of course, everyone called him David, so the request was not unreasonable, but how was she to stay immune to him when he invited familiarity? Even now, his movement toward her had caused her heart to pick up its beat. She nodded in reply and rose, unconsciously putting the chair between them.

"I'll have something by Friday... David."

"Good. Let me know if you need any help."

Hayley turned and almost reached the door when his call stopped her. "Don't forget the RFP. Can't do a thing without it."

Mortified that she could have forgotten, Hayley blushed and returned for the document in his hand. When she ventured a glance at his face, she saw a chiding, patronizing grin. She snatched the document from his fingers and fled, his low chuckle following her out the door.

In the security of her office, Hayley leaned against the door and drew a ragged breath. The man turned her inside out — serious one minute, patronizing the next, and always devastatingly attractive. How was she going to work with him during an informal proposal writing? Worse yet, how was she going to learn all she needed to know in four days? Even less. A poster on her wall showed a furry white cat gripping a horizontal tree branch with the admonition *Hang on! It's almost Friday*. Hayley groaned. Friday was a lot closer than she liked to think.

In blind panic, she started at the beginning. With Maggie's help, she gathered other proposals from the company files and retreated to her office, blinds down. She read the RFP carefully then browsed through the eight or nine proposals that had won Mansfield contracts in the past, absorbing the writing style and format. By the end of the day, she could sketch the proposal — an executive summary, a section on staffing, and detailed technical service descriptions followed by a section on finances.

When Tuesday was over, she had talked with everyone David had suggested. She had also spoken to David briefly about one procedural detail, and that interaction had convinced her that she should try to gain her knowledge elsewhere. A racing heart and sweating palms did not help a discussion of RFPs and company policies. By Wednesday, she was writing down her thoughts, organizing them into a rough outline, and had started the analysis of the number of people needed for each task. Those activities took her through to Friday morning.

After working late two nights in a row, her eyes felt like weighted stones, but her body was running on nervous energy. *This thing will fly*, Hayley thought. *But will he like my ideas? Will he accept what I've done?* His eyes saying, *"I want this,"* hovered in her mind. She finished the final presentation charts, and by one o'clock, she was waiting impatiently for one of the girls from the energy project to finish at the copier. Maggie poked her head in the room.

"There you are, Hayley. Call for you on line four."

Hayley hugged the package of paper to her chest and stormed back to the library. As she prepared to dump the paper on top of all the other paper with which she had lived for the past week, her eye caught the blinking new message icon on her computer. She clicked, and a terse notice stared up at her.

From David Mansfield to members of the PA-DEP Proposal Group:

Meeting to discuss RFP DEP35-70689 will be held at two o'clock Friday in the tenth floor conference room.

Hayley clicked Delete with a small huff then punched the line button and picked up the receiver. "Hayley Lancaster."

"Hayley! Light of my life. How is the new job?"

A bouncing voice, charged with affection, brought Hayley an instant picture of a jovial man with curling brown hair and green eyes. Her irritation swept away. Hayley laughed and sank into her chair, swirling it as she landed.

"Peter! It's good to hear from you. This is the worst time in history to be calling."

"Has Master J. D. got you working hard already? You've only been there three weeks."

"J. D.?" Hayley paused. "Oh, you mean David."

A short silence hung on the line. "David, is it?" Some of the joking left Peter's voice. "On a first-name basis already. I thought you only fell for the Jameson charm."

Hayley chose to ignore his undercurrent of seriousness. "Charm may not be the right word for the boss. Authoritative with a hefty dash of charisma, maybe. He just likes to keep things informal. By the way, how did you know his initials? He doesn't use the *J*."

The buoyancy in Peter's voice disappeared. "We're acquainted."

"And you never said a word," Hayley chided gently. "You knew I was applying here."

"I didn't want to influence your decision."

That statement was said in such a flat tone, so unlike Peter, that Hayley was immediately curious. "I don't understand."

"David and I are not on the most cordial terms," Peter said. "He *is* a business rival."

Hayley sensed there was more to the story but tried a different tack. "I didn't realize that PAJ Associates would be interested in the same kind of contracts."

"Like the DEP database thing?"

Sly devil, Hayley thought, and smiled. "You saw the RFP."

"Who hasn't? What a gem of a project! Even the small outfits will be out on this one. Will Mansfield bid?"

Hayley glanced at her watch, and her pulse jumped. "I don't know yet. There's a meeting today to discuss it, and that's where I'm supposed to be in forty-five minutes. I've really got to go."

"Does Mansfield want it?"

"Peter!" Hayley said in exasperation. "Yes, I think he does. And as in most of his business, if he knows what he wants, he'll go for it."

"So will I, if you hadn't noticed."

From Peter's teasing, Hayley knew that he had shifted the subject to a familiar theme. Ever since meeting Hayley six months ago, Peter had made it obvious he was interested in her romantically. So far, Hayley had stalled him by pleading that she needed to get her life in order and get settled in a job before she could think of serious romance. Peter had agreed to be patient but had proceeded to take her out whenever he could and present his case before her. On her side, Hayley felt warm affection, but she wasn't sure that was enough for a commitment.

"Since you've done an excellent job of showing me where you stand," Hayley answered, "let's not belabor the point. Right now, my mind is on a finicky photocopier and a presentation in—" She glanced at her watch again. "—forty minutes. Peter, please."

Laughter skipped over the line. "Okay, you win. I'll let you get back to your labor of love for J. D." Before Hayley could protest his choice of words, he continued. "But not before you promise to have dinner with me on Wednesday night. I think I've given you enough time to adjust to the new job."

At that Hayley had to laugh. "I wondered where you've been. Three weeks is a long time."

"So you missed me?"

Hayley heard the hope in his voice and answered casually. "Yes, of course, silly. So where are we going?"

"Surprise, surprise. I'll pick you up at seven-thirty. In celebration of your new job, we're going all out. Coat-and-tie kind of place."

"Wow! Now you have me waiting with bated breath." Hayley felt a sense of contentment return. It was good to joke with a friend and bask a little in his attention. No strings, no pressure. The affection she had for Peter grew just a little. "Peter?"

"Yes?"

"I promise you'll have my full attention on Wednesday, and I'll tell you all about the job."

"The prospect will keep me sane. 'Bye, Hayley."

For once the copier was free when she got to it, and Hayley shot the papers through the automatic feeder, praying that the machine would not be cruel enough to jam. She spent the last minutes reviewing important points in her mind and rechecking the copies. The clock showed a minute to two. With a hurried word to Maggie that she was going, Hayley clutched the presentation materials and took the stairs two at a time to the tenth floor.

The door to the conference room was open a crack. Hayley could hear the low rumble of voices and then a burst of laughter. Up until that moment, she had had no time for fear, but now her knees began to tremble. She counted to ten, pushed the door open, and walked in.

CHAPTER 3

Three men sat at the oval conference table. Jeff Bauer, manager of computer operations, had his usual overslept look — ruffled brown hair, rumpled shirt, and loose-and-off-center tie. In sharp contrast Pat Harlan, the systems analyst, was a dark, slender figure poured into a stylish suit and shirt. These two were deep in discussion over a computer problem that had brought the system down for most of the morning. The third man, Mathew Hempfield, lifted his hand in greeting to Hayley. "Are you ready for this?"

Hayley grinned and walked toward a seat near him. Of everyone at Mansfield Inc. who had given her advice about this RFP, Hayley liked Dr. Matt the best. He coordinated all the company projects, and she'd noticed in his interactions that he succeeded in making each staff member feel that he or she was just as important to the company as the president. Bright hazel eyes and thinning white hair gave him the look of an elderly gentleman professor, hence the title *Dr*. The fact that he held a doctorate in ecology often went unnoticed.

"My knees are shaking. But I'm as ready as I'll ever be." Hayley sat in the chair beside him and shuffled through her papers to arrange the packets she would hand around.

"You'll do fine," Dr. Matt said and patted her wrist. "I was impressed with what we discussed."

Hayley flashed him a smile. "Thanks."

The door banged open, and Eileen Kaufmann breezed in with two manila folders and a large accounting book under her arm. She sank into a chair opposite the two computer men and spoke to the room. "These taxes will never get done by the fifteenth. Especially when I haven't received all *your* expense reports." She raised her voice on the last sentence and threw the challenge toward the pair across from her.

Jeff looked up with an innocent smile. "Were you talking to me?"

"Both of you." Eileen pointed her pen at them in turn. "No later than Monday. Got that, you two?"

Pat raised his hands in surrender. "Monday. We promise. Don't we, Jeff?"

Jeff nodded. "Of course. Monday. You bet, Eileen."

The pair immediately bent their heads together, and the low drone of their conversation rolled over the table.

Eileen groaned. "I'll get the reports if I remind them once an hour today and twice on Monday," she said to Hayley. "Brilliant, but real pains, if you know what I mean."

Eileen opened the accounting book to check some figures. Sunlight flashed off the silver barrette she wore to hold her chignon in place. A classic hairstyle for a classy woman, Hayley thought, and leaned back in her chair. She checked the time. Five minutes past two. The boss was late.

Hayley's eyes strayed around the room as she strove to manage her nerves. After a few moments, her mind registered the fact that there were photographs on the walls. All were in color and grouped in themes. *People* was one theme, Hayley noted. A wedding in a Russian Orthodox church, children frolicking in the spray of an open fire hydrant, lovers walking in Schenley Park. Another group depicted festivals. Shots of the summertime Three Rivers Arts Festival, with its open-air art show and band concerts, and the Pittsburgh Folk Festival full of laughing dancers in gaily-colored ethnic costumes. Other photos included a sunrise over the Alleghenies and houses in fading Victorian splendor perched on a steep hillside far above an old church. In the collection, the photographer had managed to capture not the vision that the tourist sees in a short stay, but the essence of Pittsburgh where people lived, played, and worked. They were magnificent.

The door swung open, and David Mansfield strode in. Hayley's study of the photos broke off in the tide of energy he carried into every room he entered.

"Sorry I'm late." He noted those in attendance, and his eyes rested on the computer men, still discussing the problem. "Well, fellows, do we have a system or not?"

Pat broke off in the middle of his sentence. "We have a system, and we should have some explanation for the problem by this evening."

David nodded. "I'll be here tonight for a while and tomorrow. Let me know as soon as you can." He opened a file folder and drew out several documents. "Now to the business at hand." He sat and addressed the group. "I thought that the people in this room would be a good core to decide on the DEP proposal. You've all talked with Hayley, right?" Everyone nodded. "Good. Then why don't you start, Hayley. What did you find?"

This is it, Hayley thought. She ignored her nervous stomach and began to pass out the packets of paper.

"The materials here summarize the information that you all provided." She grinned at Dr. Matt's wink and felt her stomach unwind a notch. "Thanks for your help and your time. My first effort in RFP evaluation couldn't be here without you." Sensing that these meetings were informal, she remained seated and continued. "The first page is an outline of the main contract items which Mansfield would have to address. On each page that follows, one of the items has been restated, and Mansfield's qualifications noted. Finally, there is a tentative floor plan of the facility and a chart of manpower figures for the startup and maintenance of the operation. Since this is the first time any of you have seen the whole picture, let's run through it item by item." She glanced toward David. He was nodding slightly in agreement, and through his glasses she saw his eyes give her permission to continue. Gathering confidence from this tiny gesture and the knowledge that she knew this report intimately, Hayley proceeded to explain the points one by one.

In her nervousness, Hayley gained a sixth sense where David was concerned, and she glanced at him frequently to judge his reaction. Usually he seemed engrossed in the paper in front of him. However, when she least expected it, her eyes met his head on. At such encounters, her pulse skipped and pounded more than could be explained by nervousness alone. Only by sheer determination did Hayley succeed in stopping a trembling hand or a sharp intake of breath. If there was anything she must do, it was to hold on to the flow of the presentation.

As one of the group, David added his comments, but he allowed Hayley to steer the discussion. Only occasionally did he wield his position to bring the discussion back on track.

"What do you think about the manpower, Hayley? These figures show us to have a definite lack of qualified people."

"That will be the weakest part of our proposal," Hayley agreed. "We will need to hire at least three information professionals for acquisition and reference functions, and technical staff for materials processing. From the contractor's view, we may need more people with a background in the sciences. Dr. Matt has suggested several people who would be willing to act as consultants *and* let us use their résumés in the proposal."

"The vital combination," David quipped.

Hayley's head swung to him, her eyes bright. She was caught in David's gleaming gaze, unrestricted by his glasses, which now twirled idly in his fingers. The room brightened and shimmered in the afternoon light. Hayley found it impossible to think. The most important thing in the world at that moment was his expression — a hint of a smile topped by those glorious eyes.

"Go on, Hayley."

David's quiet words, said with just a touch of admonishment, jolted Hayley out of her trance. "Right. Where was I? Oh, yes, professionals." Hayley took a breath to steady her voice. "Although we don't have the people now, the job market in the information field is fairly tight, and I personally know several recent library-school graduates who would fit the qualifications."

"Pat, what about the DEP computer farm? Can it handle this?"

That question from David allowed Hayley a moment to give herself a mental shake. Why did he always make her feel like a Mack truck out of control?

After Pat finished, a comfortable silence fell in the room. David leafed through the report until he came to the floor plan. He looked up at Hayley. "Where did this come from?"

"We will be using government office space, and the RFP gives room dimensions. I made some assumptions about the shape of the rooms and assessed whether the operation could be done in the space. From what I know now, it can."

"Good, good. It's well-known that government office space is not always up to specifications. At least, we won't be working in a closet. Any other comments?" He waited a full minute for an answer then said, "Shall we bid?"

With that small question, Hayley realized that the company was actually accepting her work and was planning to take on the responsibility of writing a proposal and possibly carrying it out. Pride welled up in her as she watched the general nodding of heads.

"All right, then. Hayley—" He paused until her head turned to him. "—good job."

In those two words, Hayley heard the praises of Caesar and the blare of trumpets. "Thanks", she managed to whisper and heard the group's general concurrence through a blur of emotions. The mention of her name brought her back to the discussion.

"Hayley will be responsible for the bulk of the writing concerning the basic database and information center plans," David was saying. "She'll need backup from you two." He motioned to Pat and Jeff. "Eileen, you'll do the financial statements with me. Dr. Matt, work with Hayley on the personnel section and those all-important résumés. I'll write the company intro and help Hayley pull it all together. Any questions?"

Again, a significant pause, not for effect, Hayley realized, but a real chance for questions to be raised. "All right, that's all for today."

Chairs bumped along the carpet as the group prepared to leave.

"Oh, one more thing," David said, breaking into the small talk. "Since we have a new staff member on board, this is a good time to remind you all that from this point on, the proposal is company confidential. This proposal should not be discussed with anyone outside the company, and all paperwork should be locked up when not in use. If you haven't changed your computer password in the past week, do it now. I want to see the first drafts on my desk by next Friday." He then nodded his dismissal.

Hayley lingered. She had been under a microscope for more than two hours, and the retreating nervous energy left mental exhaustion in its wake. She gathered up papers and stacked them in a pile. All the others had left, but David was still poring over the papers and making notes. Hayley shook her head and continued her own organization. Seeing that he was probably not leaving any time soon, Hayley said quietly, "If I don't see you, have a good weekend, David."

He gave her his attention at that and rose, moving smoothly around the edge of the table, hand outstretched. "I wanted to congratulate you again. That was an excellent presentation. I do like to—" He broke off as Hayley took his hand. "Your hands are like ice!" He took the other hand to confirm the discovery and gently rubbed her fingers with his broad palms. A shot of pleasure launched through Hayley's hands and warmed her. She felt a blush rise in her cheeks and looked down at her hands.

"It's not cold in here," David said, confusion in his voice.

Hayley laughed nervously and pulled her hands from his grasp. To her, the room had become close and hot. The urge to escape the now familiar riot of emotions that David's presence always caused bubbled to the surface. "It's nothing," she said lightly. "When I'm nervous, the blood drains from my hands, and they get cold. It happens when I'm excited, too." She turned to grasp the back of the chair.

"And what were you today… nervous or excited?"

By this time, she had controlled the shiver of her spine and looked at him. "Nervous. Very."

"Really? You seemed to have everything under control."

If you only knew, Hayley thought.

"As I was saying before I had the pleasure of warming your hands…" Hayley's eyes shot to his. Their darkened color confirmed that the contact had affected him, too. David continued. "…I like to interview all applicants for permanent positions in the company. This time, I'm glad I trusted Maggie's judgment. You're going to be an asset."

Hayley flushed again. "Thanks." Would she ever be able to thank him above a whisper? she wondered.

David slipped his hands in his pockets. "As a reward, I'd like you to go to DEP's Industry Day with me."

Hayley drew her brows together. "Industry Day?"

"It's a meeting offered by a government agency for all the companies in the local area that might be interested in working with that agency in the future. Anyone planning to bid on the current RFP will get a private interview to ask questions. It seems DEP is planning on holding the Day in the proposed office space. Since you've done so much of the preliminary work, you might as well be there."

"Doesn't sound like much of a reward to me."

David smiled. "It's work, but it does get you out of the office for an afternoon." When Hayley made no comment and regarded him skeptically, he added with a devilish expression, "They usually serve crackers and cheese."

With a laugh, Hayley threw up her hands. "That settles it. Of course I'll go."

David joined her laughter with a chuckle. "Good. Industry Day is on Monday. Louise can give you the details."

He stood only a foot away from her, his hands still in his pockets, waiting. But waiting for what? Studying the floor for a few moments, he then met her questioning gaze. "I… well, I'll see you on Monday, then." He stumbled over the words.

"Sure. See you Monday." Hayley quickly loaded the pile of papers into her arms and headed for the door.

"Have a good weekend, Hayley." His voice caused her to shiver.

"You, too", she said, and left before any more silence came between them. Silence that murmured persuasively. At any rate, if she was going to talk to Louise, Hayley knew she had better hurry. It was four-thirty now, and Louise left at five on the dot on Friday. Hayley walked to the front office and slid into one of the armchairs.

In a reflex built from practice, Louise glanced up from her typing then continued until the sentence was finished. She swiveled to face Hayley and asked an eagerly, "So, how did it go?"

"Very well," Hayley said. "Everything I recommended was accepted, except for some details. I can live with it."

"Terrific."

"David even complimented me," Hayley continued, catching Louise's pleased look. "And he asked me to go to Industry Day with him."

Louise smiled slyly. "Then he *was* pleased. I suggested that he take you."

"You did?"

Louise brushed Hayley's surprise aside. "Of course. I knew when you were working on the presentation that you ought to be in on everything, and I told David. He always wants to write the proposals by himself, but to tell you the truth, he needs an extra head. I'm glad he asked."

"He said you'd give me the details about the conference."

Louise nodded. "I'll forward the meeting invite to you from David's calendar. At these meetings, everyone's competing against everyone else. The idea is to be friendly, say very little about your own company and proposal, and find out as much as possible about everyone else's. Simple, really, once you get the hang of it."

Hayley laughed. "Simple. Right."

"Let's see. What else?" Louise tapped her pen against the desk blotter. "David will drive; I think he's planning to leave at one o'clock. Take your notes and questions and be prepared to absorb all you can. That's all I can think of."

"Thanks," Hayley said. She rose from the chair and another thought struck her. "Louise, who did the photographs in the conference room? They're sensational."

"David did them. They are good, aren't they?" She leaned back in the chair, arms crossed. "You know, I asked him once if he were going to do any more. He said he didn't have time." She pursed her lips. "I tend to think he stopped after the accident."

"Accident?"

Louise eyes widened, then she smiled. "Well, of course, you wouldn't know. About five years ago, David's car was hit head-on by a drunk driver. He spent two months in the hospital and limped a long time after that. His wife was killed instantly."

The fact that David had been seriously injured brought an exclamation to Hayley's throat; the fact that he had been married forced the sound back. She could only imagine the pain, both physical and emotional, that he must have suffered. "It must have been difficult for him," she said simply.

Louise shrugged, "I really don't know. I met him almost six months after the accident, and by then he had himself well in hand. Of course, he never talks about Julia — his wife — or the accident, but I'm sure the scars are there. The photography was the most obvious victim."

The telephone buzzed. Louise pressed the intercom button and answered, "This is Louise... Thanks, Joyce." She pressed the flashing light on the phone as she motioned for Hayley to stay a moment. "Louise Whitney." She listened then said, "Do you have any idea when the shipment will be in?"

Hayley could tell by Louise's frown that this call was going to be lengthy and probably not pleasant. Hayley tapped Louise on the shoulder and mouthed, "Have a good weekend."

She closed the office door behind her and walked back to the library.

In her office, the first thing she saw was a note pinned to the upholstery of her chair.

Hayley: Hope the meeting went well. Got a hot date. Close up for me.

Thanks. Maggie.

Hayley carefully filed all the papers from the proposal and locked her file cabinet. Just that morning Maggie had mentioned that someone had made a sweep of the graphics room, stealing every pen and tool that wasn't locked up. Taken in light of David's warning this afternoon, *company confidential* could not be taken too seriously.

After locking the file cabinet, Hayley sat behind her desk and typed up a to-do list for Monday, mentally reviewing the day to determine what would be most pressing. She changed her password before shutting down. Then walking slowly through the library, she shut down computers, locked the doors, and turned off lights.

Her thoughts ran over the hours she had spent preparing the presentation and the surge of pride she had experienced when David complimented her. Warmth stole over her as she remembered David's hands over hers gently rubbing until the blood returned to her fingers. The memory shifted to a collage of her other encounters with the boss.

Why was it so hard to stay in control when he was around? *Stupid question*, she answered herself. He was handsome. *Without a doubt*, her objective side piped in. Competent. *Again, no question.* Sensitive. *In his photographs, at least.* Committed. *To the company, maybe not to anything else.* Had he been committed to Julia? Could he be committed to someone again?

Hayley! her rational voice argued. *If you're not careful, you'll find yourself in a most awkward situation. Getting involved with the boss is not safe unless you know he feels something, too. You have a massive crush on the man, that's all. You can handle that.*

Now that she had identified the upheavals her body performed in David's presence, Hayley answered her voice aloud, "Without a doubt." She walked back to her office and pulled her sweater off the coat rack. Deliberately ignoring the giddiness that had surfaced just thinking of David Mansfield, she shut the door behind her with a solid thud.

As she turned off the last lights in the library and made a final check of the room, she repeated to herself in quiet litany, "No problem. I can handle a crush. No problem at all."

CHAPTER 4

When Hayley first saw the building where the DEP had rented office space, her heart skipped in delight. The flavor of old-world business pervaded the elevator caged in wrought iron. The hallway on the fifteenth floor shone with new wax, as did the paneling that reached halfway up the walls. Opulent pink marble topped the paneling to complete the aura of sophistication.

Then she and David entered the DEP suite, and Hayley grimaced. Gray steel desks and chairs stood on a carpet of industrial army green. Nail holes pockmarked walls painted a shade lighter than the furniture. Standing in the reception area in a tailored suit the color of spring lilacs, Hayley felt like a splash of paint on a black-and-white photograph.

With her tablet computer case positioned comfortably under her arm, Hayley followed David toward the center of the room. She stopped to pick up a plastic glass filled with a transparent pink liquid and sampled a few diamond-shaped crackers from the refreshment table. The liquid turned out to be watered-down wine punch, and the crackers were stale. *At least the place has windows*, she thought.

Given that the drizzly sky matched the color of the walls, the unadorned windows only added to the depressing atmosphere. When David motioned to her from his position near one of the office doors, Hayley gratefully dropped the remaining crackers in the trash and moved through the buzzing crowd to join him and the man by his side. Slicked-back, black hair and dark, gleaming eyes suggested that David's companion had bathed in oil.

"Hayley, I'd like you to meet Simon Ross," David said. "Simon, Hayley Lancaster. Simon's the contracting officer for DEP. As I was saying, Hayley is an information specialist at Mansfield."

"Nice to meet you, Mr. Ross," Hayley said and held out her hand. A wet paw engulfed her fingers, and the slimy gaze accompanying the grip made her stomach curl.

Covering Hayley's hand with his other paw, Simon leaned toward her and said, "I'm delighted to meet one of David's associates. How do you like working at Mansfield?"

"I'm enjoying it," Hayley answered and strove not to wipe her hands on her skirt when Simon released her. Her relief ended when she felt a fleshy hand on her elbow.

"Good, good," Simon said, squeezing her elbow. "We need to keep our employees happy, eh, Dave?" He winked broadly toward David.

In her struggle to maintain her composure under Simon's attentions, Hayley had forgotten David's presence. Now the low, hard tone of his voice surprised her.

"We certainly do, and it looks like this employee needs another glass of punch. Good to see you again, Simon."

With a glance at the glint in David's eyes, Hayley took her cue and moved out of Simon's reach. "Nice to meet you", she said.

David's hand in the small of her back propelled her toward the refreshment table. "The man's a snake," he muttered.

"He's harmless enough." Hayley laughed lightly. "Guys like that aren't worth even a passing notice."

They had almost reached the table. "He will be if we win the contract," David said. "Keeping him at bay while running this project could be a major headache."

Shock rippled through Hayley. She turned to David to ask him if he meant that *she* would run the project. She had barely learned proposal writing, let alone project management. Before she could speak, two more potential bidders joined them, greeting David with contrived enthusiasm. Hayley made a mental note to ask him later and concentrated on the activity around her.

David shielded his own information while deftly probing his competitors, a technique she could use. A few questions were put to her once she had been introduced, but remembering Louise's warnings and listening to David, she gave noncommittal answers with a bright smile.

Hayley noticed a stocky, balding man heading in their direction. She touched David on the sleeve.

When he recognized the man, David's face broke into a pleased grin. "Mick, good to see you." The two shook hands.

"You, too, David. I assume you're in the running, and you'll assume I am, so that's out of the way. Always like to know the best is in the competition."

"Thanks, Mick. That was magnanimous coming from you."

Mick ignored the sarcasm and turned to Hayley, his eyes bright with anticipation. "I came over solely to get an introduction."

In the brief pause that followed, Hayley sensed David stiffen beside her.

Just when she was about to break the silence, David spoke. "Hayley Lancaster, this is Mick Kaminsky. He runs a shop in North Hills."

Without waiting for a response from Hayley, Mick took her hand in both of his. "Call me Mick. And the pleasure is all mine. David, my boy, where have you been hiding this one?" Mick questioned with a twinkle in his brown eyes that stared out under heavy eyelids. He clasped her hand more tightly than Hayley felt was proper, but there seemed to be no way to back away without obvious rudeness.

With careful enunciation, David said, "If you can keep your wolfish instincts under control for just a minute, Mick, I will explain that Hayley is an information specialist at Mansfield. She's been doing background research on the RFP."

Unabashed by David's less-than-cordial reprimand, Mick dropped Hayley's hand and smiled. "My apologies," he said, throwing a look at David as if to judge his reaction. "I should have realized that you were not among David's usual style of woman. I keep hoping he will find someone to fill the loneliness in his life and leave the field clear for the rest of us."

David answered crisply, "Sorry, Mick. I'm still in that competition, too."

Mick stepped back from Hayley as if she were hot. Hayley glanced at David for some clarification of Mick's movement and saw him shoot a silent warning look at Mick.

Baffled by such a hostile expression from David, Hayley spoke up to ease the sudden strain. "I just came on board." In her nervous breathlessness, her voice sounded a tone higher than normal. "Mr. Mansfield brought me along so I could learn what Industry Day is like."

Mick followed the intended direction and slipped his hands into his pockets. "What have you found out so far?"

Hayley told him about putting faces to names of the companies that she had heard mentioned, but half her attention was on the simmering man beside her. That warning glance to Mick along with David's words implied that David considered Hayley part of the *competition*. No, that was ridiculous. Just because *she* felt like a teenager with a first crush didn't mean that David felt the same way.

After a few more inconsequential remarks, Mick excused himself, leaving Hayley and David alone in the crowd. She started to turn to David when he snapped in an undertone, "You'd think this was a cocktail party instead of a business gathering. I should have left you at the office."

After a moment of shock at David's vehemence, a searing fury flared up so swiftly in Hayley that her hands shook. *Just like a man*, she seethed inwardly. *Quick to judge the woman but not other men.* She drew herself up to the limit of her height and threw her empty glass in the trashcan at her side.

"I'm sorry I cramp your style," she hissed. "Next time, find someone who'll cause you less trouble." She'd swung away from him and had taken two steps toward the door when her arm was gripped from behind. David spun her around to face him.

His eyes, so shortly before dark with anger, were exasperated. "I'm sorry," he said.

Hayley heard the words but no apology. She looked pointedly at his hand. Instantly, he dropped it, all anger wiped from his face. This time the apology rang in a tone rich with regret. "I'm sorry. I didn't mean…"

He reached out for her arm, and Hayley stepped back. She saw a flash of hurt fly through his eyes. The room seemed to fade as they stood looking at each other, a jumble of feelings running between them. The air vibrated with unspoken communication.

Hayley whispered, "I'll leave now."

David reached for her again but drew back before touching her. "No, please," he said quickly, then took another breath. "I'm angry with myself for not warning you about these meetings and for not being better prepared myself. You should not have to put up with marauding animals. If you want to go back to the office, go ahead, but I still need you here. I would like you to stay."

David's protectiveness warmed Hayley. Although his request sounded professional, a voice within her hinted that the request might be personal. But she would take what was given, not what she'd hoped would be offered.

"Apology accepted."

This time his hand did reach her arm, and his soft touch melted her as thoroughly as his sharp words had hurt earlier.

"They're starting the introduction," Dave murmured with a smile that contained the remainder of the apology. "We'd better take our seats."

The room and its noise returned to Hayley's consciousness. She nodded and let him guide her to the metal folding chairs set before a projection screen and overhead projector. Throughout the presentation, when Simon Ross brought up something that David felt was important, he leaned toward Hayley and softly explained the significance of the information to the contract plans. Hayley found herself whispering questions to him and receiving clear, precise answers. Once he asked her if a particular DEP procedure made sense, and when she voiced her negative opinion, David nodded in agreement. He treated her as an equal, a business associate — nothing more, nothing less. It was a comfortable exchange, thankfully free of the stronger emotions of previous encounters. In this calmer atmosphere, Hayley could forget David's previous behavior and bask in business equality.

When the lights came up and the final words were spoken, the attendees broke into groups for a tour of the facilities. David suggested that they separate. "I have my one-on-one with Simon. We'll compare notes later," he said. "And remember, don't be afraid to ask general questions about the local operation here in Pittsburgh. That's what this session is for."

Hayley nodded, and David moved to join a group near the projection screen. Hayley looked around and noticed a waving hand in a group gathering at the door to her left.

Peter Jameson was only an inch taller than Hayley but seemed bigger because of his stout frame. From the top of his curling brown hair to the tips of his shining wing-tip shoes, he projected the image of a teddy bear with a very good valet. The gray suit fit him well, and the handkerchief peeking from the breast pocket was just the right touch for the successful businessman. Hayley returned the smile that she knew was especially for her and wished that David would smile at her like that just once. Horrified by her stray thought, she forced a brighter smile on her lips and took Peter's outstretched hands with a show of pleasure.

"What are you doing here?" she asked.

Peter grinned. "Same as you, I would imagine."

"So you *are* going to bid on this. After we talked on Friday, I wondered."

"PAJ Associates is into anything that will make a little money without much effort. This is one of those. What about Mansfield? How did your meeting go?"

"I think we'll bid," she said slowly, not sure if this admission came under the heading of company confidential. But most people gave out that kind of information, so she thought she was safe.

Conversation around them evaporated as the group moved off behind a DEP employee acting as their guide. Reminded of her reason for being at the conference, Hayley flipped open her writing case, positioned it across her arm for a writing surface, and scribbled notes on offices.

During a lull in the running commentary, Peter whispered, "Where's David?"

"One-on-one," Hayley whispered back while still writing. "I'll meet him back in the front room."

"Do we still have a date on Wednesday?"

That brought her eyes to his. "Of course," she said with a grin.

After the tour was over and they were walking back to the reception area, Peter compared the tour guide to a fabled government worker who had accumulated so much paperwork on her desk that when her retirement papers had finally come, they had instantly disappeared in the confusion. She had been forced to remain in the job a full year before the papers surfaced. With difficulty, Hayley stifled some unladylike giggles, and when Peter took her hand, she leaned onto his shoulder to muffle the laugh.

"Something for all of us to know?"

Hayley stopped short at the cold voice that moved like a glacier over the merriment she had been sharing with Peter. Still holding Peter's hand, she raised her head. A chill slithered down her arms. David's blue eyes glittered at Peter with untarnished hate. Hayley squeezed Peter's hand. The smile so wide just seconds ago had frozen.

"Just my old government paperwork story," Peter said in a steady voice. "You know the one."

Under David's intense gaze, Hayley moved a step away from Peter and dropped his hand. David replied with less malice, but no less coldness, "You shouldn't trap every unsuspecting person with it."

Peter visibly relaxed. "I know when I have an appreciative audience."

"You've met, then?"

"Oh, yes," Peter replied with a knowing grin at Hayley.

Hayley watched the scene in silence. Peter had said on the phone that he and David were business rivals, but a little competition did not explain David's fighting stance. In fact, Hayley noticed that David's hands clenched and unclenched at his side as if he were debating the consequences of landing a good punch.

Those consequences were never tested. A muscular man with tawny hair set his impressive frame between the two men and addressed Peter. "I got those figures you wanted."

Peter eyed the man as if he were coming out of a trance. "What? Oh, yes. Thanks, Carl," he said, and took the papers out of the man's hand.

The tense silence lasted only a breath this time. When the newcomer spoke to David, Hayley suspected that the interruption had been deliberate.

"David, good to see you again."

David took the outstretched hand with a curt nod. "Hello, Carl."

The man addressed Hayley. "I don't believe we've met. I'm Carlton Jones. I work with Peter over at PAJ."

The chill in the air warmed to coolness under the presence of this man who, Hayley guessed, approached every situation in the same way — straight on. In this case she was more than happy for his intervention.

"Hayley Lancaster. I'm an information specialist at Mansfield." She noted as she released Carlton's hand that Peter and David were still eyeing each other warily, and she wondered if another skirmish would start. To Hayley's dismay, Peter threw down the next gauntlet.

"Carl will probably be managing this project," he said with a gleam in his eyes.

"You have to win first, Jameson," David countered with decided calm.

Peter's smile widened. "We'll see, won't we?" Then, dismissing David, he said, "Carl, we'd better get back to the office. Can't party all afternoon." He pressed Hayley's shoulder. "I'll see you later, okay?"

"Sure," Hayley answered, aware of the sudden stillness in her boss after Peter's parting words. She had hoped that Peter's departure would soften David's manner but soon realized her error. David now moved stiffly through the crowd making the last rounds of the room, his words curt. He kept a firm hand on Hayley's elbow and guided her adroitly around groups of people, out into the hall and into the elevator. He shut the elevator cage with a vicious clang. They rode down in silence.

When David finally spoke, it was the last thing in the world Hayley expected. "How long have you known Peter Jameson?"

No apology. No explanation. Just… an accusation.

"What?" Hayley shot back.

"You heard me. How long have you known him?"

"After your caveman routine back there, you have the nerve to ask me something like that? I don't think it's any of your business."

"It is if there is a possibility that confidential material could find its way into a competitor's office."

In a flash, Hayley caught the inference. Her temper flared. "You're way out of line, David. I'm not sure what you have against Peter, but you don't know me well enough to include me in your disagreement. Your accusation is ridiculous." She swallowed once then said, "I expect an apology."

David turned the full power of his gaze on her, judging her, questioning her. But he said nothing.

The elevator door slid open. David yanked the cage door open and strode away from Hayley into the parking garage. She stood motionless, staring after him, her body trembling in anger and bewilderment. The elevator door began to close, and she hurried through, watching as it opened again momentarily, then closed. She took a deep breath and looked around. David was nowhere in sight.

So much the better, she thought. She needed a few moments to deal with the volcano of confusion brewing inside.

The low purr of an engine to her left caused Hayley to turn and see the blue sedan in which they had arrived. David leaned over the seat and pushed the door open from the inside. Hayley walked to the car and got in with an air of calm she hoped would be convincing. She settled in the seat, made a great show of buckling her seat belt, and stared straight ahead. Without a word, David guided the car through the maze of lanes and out into the dull, dripping weather.

Hayley's mind raced through details of the elevator encounter, wondering why David had acted the way he had. As her mind slowed, Hayley hazarded a glance toward the driver. David's hands squeezed the wheel, and his shoulders hunched forward. At one traffic light, he looked her way as if sensing her contemplation and rubbed his hands against the wheel while forcing his shoulders to relax.

The light changed, and David drove on. The silence continued until they arrived at the parking garage under their office building. Hayley's thoughts flew through the consequences of the afternoon. What would she do if he didn't apologize? What if he did? In any case, this situation could not continue. She would have to quit. She wouldn't be the subject of insensitive judgments from a lout of a boss. Even if he was handsome. Even if he intrigued her and excited her more than any man she had ever met. Even if…

The car halted in a parking space. Hayley thrust the door open. Before she could swing out, David's voice stopped her.

"Please. Wait." As rough as his voice had been in the elevator, now it was soft. Behind those two words lay a wealth of pleading. She turned to face him and saw a deep weariness edged into his features. He did not look at her but focused on a concrete support outside the car. Hayley pulled the door shut.

"You're right, of course," he said. "I'm sorry. For the accusation… and for my behavior. I don't make a habit of bullying my employees at meetings or in elevators." He rubbed the back of his neck absently then turned to face her. His eyes reflected a sense of awe. "In fact, this is the first time." His fingers reached forward and gently brushed her cheek. "I don't know what it is about you—" He broke off and resumed his study of the concrete.

With the wisdom of hindsight, Hayley could readily believe that this had, indeed, been the first time he had transgressed his own boundaries. According to other employees she'd talked to, his saintly qualities included a strict observance of business proprieties. What could have made him lose control? What could have made him so protective early in the afternoon and so angry with Peter later? Unless... unless he was attracted to her. Hayley looked at David's silent profile while her heart took wings. Could she dare hope that?

"At any rate," David continued, "I am sorry. It won't happen again. You're right about Peter." He shook his head. "Our quarrel should not influence how I deal with you. I have no evidence that you would deliberately jeopardize this proposal. But it has happened before. Two years ago, one of my employees was dating a woman from Randall Computer Systems, and it cost me a contract."

In the pause that followed, several pieces of the puzzle fell into place in Hayley's mind. He was worried about the company. He was also attracted to an employee who had some relationship with a business rival. No wonder his behavior was erratic where she was concerned. Hayley thought to reassure him of her integrity, but David sighed deeply and continued.

"And I'm sensitive about Peter Jameson. You see, before she died, my wife and Peter had an affair."

CHAPTER 5

During the next two days, between conversations with team members and bouts of writing, Hayley had more than enough time to compare what she knew of Peter with David's perception. Each time she thought she could believe David — based solely on the strength of his conviction — she pictured Peter's playful eyes without a hint of malice in them. As she had in the car, Hayley repeated to herself, "It can't be true," and saw in her mind David shaking his head in a way that was both chiding and mournful.

By five o'clock on Wednesday afternoon, Hayley had given her mind some peace by deciding to ask Peter his side of the story. She had to know the truth. She glowered at the unfinished manpower figures in front of her and then at the clock. There just weren't enough hours in the day.

Maggie's head popped in her door. "Aren't you going out?"

"Yes," Hayley answered in an exasperated voice.

"Then, go!" Maggie urged. "This will be here tomorrow. I guarantee it."

"You know, you're right." Hayley stood up and shuffled the papers into uneven piles so that she could remember where she left off. "What I need is some diversion."

Maggie grinned. "And who's the lucky guy supplying said diversion?"

"Peter Jameson." Hayley looked at Maggie, and her hands stopped their motion. Maggie's eyes held an almost silly expression of surprise.

Trying to read the look, Hayley offered, "PAJ Associates?"

"Yes, I know." Maggie crossed her arms and leaned against the doorframe. The surprise vanished behind a serious, questioning gaze. "Does David know?"

An icicle of nervousness froze in Hayley's back, and she rubbed her arms against the sudden cold. "He doesn't know about this particular date, I imagine, but he does know I'm seeing Peter."

Maggie nodded thoughtfully. "And he didn't say anything to you?"

Hayley laughed. The cold prevented the sound from being pleasant. She remembered the hot anger in the elevator and the final words in the car. She shrugged off the memories. "Oh, he said plenty. I told him he had nothing to worry about. Peter and I are just friends, and I don't discuss business outside the office. With anyone."

"As long as David knows, you should be all right," Maggie said. "But be careful. Peter has been known to take advantage of his relationships where business is concerned."

Hayley nodded. "I'll keep it in mind." She checked her watch and gasped. "I'll just make the bus if I run." She grabbed her purse and sweater and bolted for the door. "Lock up, will you?"

"The way you're going, I don't have much choice," Maggie said, laughing.

At that, Hayley threw her a big smile and waved. "Thanks. See you in the morning."

About thirty minutes later, Hayley stepped off the bus in another world. Oakland was a collage of old homes and small specialty stores as well as brick and steel hospitals and condominiums, and the weathered stone of university campuses.

She glanced at her watch. Only an hour before Peter arrived. Hayley quickly walked the block and a half to her apartment building. Surrounded by period houses with gingerbread fronts and gothic columns, the squat, yellow brick structure looked like a brash teenager with bleached hair among elderly matrons. Still, it was comfortable and cheap — prime qualifications for housing on a student budget.

Hayley jabbed her key into the mailbox and tugged the letters and flyers out. She took the stairs to the second floor two at a time and burst into her apartment, flinging her purse and sweater to the table.

For a moment, her eyes ran over the living room, then she moved to action.

She plumped the needlework pillows on the wicker chairs and couch and swept the pile of *National Geographic* magazines off the round, wicker coffee table. On her way to the bookshelves, she pulled the oval rag rug back into shape with her foot. After shoving the magazines on a shelf, she twirled the rod of the mauve blinds until the setting sun cast only gentle, warming rays onto the patchwork tapestry hanging on the opposite wall. She checked the rubber plant for dust. Then, passing the ferns on the way to the bedroom, she turned each of them so the dead leaves were hidden and picked up a robe and a pair of socks from the floor.

Dumping everything on the bed, Hayley concentrated on a quick shower and change of clothes. A rose-colored dress, with a full skirt and beaded bodice, helped to replace boring manpower figures with a sense of anticipation. She was blowing her hair dry and coaxing the curls into a soft cloud around her head when a knock sounded. Finishing her appearance with silver earrings and bracelet, she went to the door.

For the evening, Peter had chosen a black three-piece suit, and when Hayley noticed the gold cuff links and tie tack, she knew he intended this to be a special night. An uneasy thought crossed her mind. He might have more on his mind than just celebrating a new job, and she tensed. After letting him into the apartment, she ignored the uneasiness and said lightly, "You're on time as usual. Can I get you a drink before we go?"

Peter's eyes lingered on her then he pulled Hayley into his arms. "The way you look, I might forget dinner altogether."

Hayley forced herself to accept the embrace with a relaxed stance. She drew away smoothly leaving her hands at his waist. "Where are we going for dinner?" she asked.

"Oh, yes…" Peter mumbled into her hair. He kissed her brow. "…I made reservations downtown." He kissed her cheek then finally stepped away with a reluctant grin. "I guess we'd better go now."

Hayley clasped his hands and kissed him back, when her mind suddenly noted, *Why bother? When you know you'd rather kiss...* She firmly shut off the thought by saying, "I'll get my coat."

The restaurant lived up to the anticipation built by Peter's cuff links. The gold leaf on the walls was no more impressive than the corps of waiters — one to explain the menu, one to fill the water glasses, one to introduce the breads, one to clear away each course. Hayley tried to act as nonchalant as all the other guests in the dining room with their high style and jewels, but she couldn't suppress an occasional sigh or exclamation.

The sommelier arrived with the wine, an imported white. Peter tasted the small portion glistening in the glass then nodded. When the glasses were filled, he lifted his to Hayley. "To your new job."

"To the job," Hayley said and touched her glass to his.

"Now tell me about it."

Hayley folded her arms on the table and leaned toward him. "At first, I wasn't sure I'd like it. I was doing boring things. Learning the library routine, cleaning out files. But Maggie sent me to work on this proposal, and it's been a real education."

"Maggie?"

"Margaret Davies, the library manager. She's a good teacher. I would never have thought of all the things a company has to consider before a bid. And information and data has to be collected for every aspect. You have to consider how much a procedure will cost, does the company have the right people, is there enough capital—"

"Is there?" Peter broke in.

Hayley studied him. "Is there what?"

"Enough capital. You do know, don't you?"

Hayley sat back and played with the rim of the wineglass. Maggie had warned her, but she still had not expected Peter's question. "I wouldn't tell you if I did." Her voice reflected the coldness that gripped her stomach.

Peter smiled then sipped his wine. "No, I didn't think you would."

The waiter arrived with steaming shrimp bisque. While he fussed over the serving, Hayley felt hot anger rise in her throat. In a series of mental snapshots, she remembered David's warnings and Maggie's skepticism. She spoke in a low tone. "Is that why you brought me here? To soften me up so I would give you some kind of information?"

Instantly Peter's hand engulfed hers. "No... Hayley, no. I wanted to see you and celebrate your new job. Honestly. It was a stupid thing to ask."

"But old habits die hard, right?"

Peter grinned sheepishly. "I just couldn't pass up the chance. But you know the game, and now I know where you stand. It reinforces my good opinion of you. I swear I won't bring the subject up again. Forgive me?"

Hayley knew she could not resist the pleading in his voice. The Industry Day meeting had taught her about the competitiveness of the business and revealed the level of scheming that went on in hallways, at parties, and, it seemed, in restaurants. She couldn't blame Peter for trying. At any rate, she was too delighted that he had brought her to this elegant restaurant to harbor a grudge. As long as he didn't push the issue.

"All right. I forgive you. But no more, Peter."

He lifted his hands in surrender. "No more. I promise. Cross my heart." He crossed his chest in the childhood sign, and Hayley broke into unsophisticated giggles, which she promptly suppressed when the busboy paused at the table. From then on, the strain eased, and through the remainder of the meal, conversation stayed strictly away from business.

By the time coffee and a strawberry torte were served, Hayley felt comfortable enough to broach the topic that had been on her mind since Monday. She began in her most nonthreatening voice. "Peter, I need to ask you a question. It's something that's been bothering me ever since the DEP meeting."

"Ask away."

"Why is there so much rivalry, so much... animosity between you and David?"

Peter's first reaction was silence — a long, measured pause that convinced Hayley that he would not answer at all.

"Have you talked to David?" he asked quietly.

"Some," Hayley admitted, wanting to be as truthful as possible without hurting Peter. "But I don't think I've heard the whole story."

Peter nodded, picked up a spoon, and stirred sugar into his coffee. "Probably not. If you want to hear about the whole sad affair, I'll tell you."

"Please."

With a deep breath, Peter began. "David and I met while we were working for a company called Cathcart & Sons on Wood Street. I did a lot of programming for them. David was — still is — a talented systems analyst. We were both new to town, so we ran around together. Played handball regularly. Sometimes double-dated. At Cathcart, David had worked himself into project management and had his eye on one of the executive positions. Then he met Julia."

Peter sipped his coffee. "She was the executive secretary for a vice president at Weston Oil, and he met her while managing one of Cathcart's contracts for them. David never dated much, but when he fell, he fell hard. He went after Julia with the same concentration I had seen him use in cracking a tough systems problem. I was best man at their wedding.

"After the honeymoon in the Bahamas, David went back to work on a more moderate schedule. Of course, he had been putting in sixty or seventy hours per week, so moderation still meant a lot of overtime. We still got together, but not as often. David said there was no reason to sever a good friendship. Julia saw it differently."

Hayley had eaten all of her torte without tasting any of it. Now she laid down her fork. "She was jealous?"

Peter nodded. "I've come to the conclusion that Julia's need for adoration was her one flaw. David doted on her, but his work was important, too. I know she tried to make David cut back on his hours. He did as much as he could, but you've seen how it is. When there's a problem or a crisis on a contract, an all-night haul may be the only way out of the mess."

Hayley nodded as she remembered bleary-eyed programmers and data-entry specialists who had stayed most of the night to re-establish data from a backup when a cranky computer had a memory lapse.

"Once she had altered his work schedule," Peter continued, "Julia turned on me, the only other significant demand on David's time. I'll give him credit — David told her to back off. The argument ripped him apart, but we still met. Then Julia started showing up unexpectedly. On the pretense of delivering contract material, she would stop in the office and make a point of talking with me. She'd offer to pick David up after handball and be delightfully pleasant. Well, it was easy to see that David was relieved, so I ignored the little bells in my head. One night, to my astonishment, she showed up at my apartment. She was worried about David. He was working so hard. Maybe I could help. We talked for about an hour or so, then she left."

The waiter poured more coffee and cleared Hayley's dessert plate. She could guess where the story was headed. The woman was a barracuda!

"This kind of thing happened every other week, then every week. After a couple of months, I told her there was really nothing I could do about David and not to come anymore. She sulked, but agreed. That was on a Wednesday."

"And so far, David had no idea she was seeing you?"

"Sure, we talked about it. But Cathcart was knee-deep in work, and David had a lot on his mind."

Now Hayley could see that Peter's whole body had stiffened beneath the suit. He cut a piece of torte but laid the fork down immediately. "The following Friday, I was at a Cathcart party, some PR bash for our customers. David stormed in with Julia trailing behind, with that little smug smile plastered on her face. He asked me to step outside." Peter shook his head. "To this day, I can't remember David's exact words. The bottom line was that he accused me of sleeping with Julia."

Hayley's eyes widened. "How did he come to that conclusion?"

"That's the story she told him. And someone had seen her leave my place. I couldn't deny that we had been meeting. I'd told him. I tried to explain. I told him I'd never touched her, but the more I talked, the angrier he got, and he hit me. Before I could get off the ground, he grabbed Julia's arm — she had followed to make sure everything she had planned was working — pushed her into the car, and tore off. That was the last time I saw her alive."

"The accident?" Hayley whispered in horror.

Peter nodded. "After David got out of the hospital, I tried to talk with him, but he was too hurt and full of guilt to listen. He quit Cathcart and started Mansfield Inc. I quit soon after he did, and here we are. I win one contract — he wins the next. So far, we're evenly matched." The lightness Peter tried to inject into the last statements failed.

Hayley watched as Peter polished off the rest of the torte and drained his cup. The waiter had taken the check and payment before Hayley could speak. "You miss that friendship, don't you?"

Peter's eyes shot up to meet hers. After a moment, he nodded. "It's hard to lose a brother."

An overwhelming sadness grew in Hayley. Sadness for a relationship lost because of an obsessive woman. She vowed she would never come between her husband and his friends.

Peter's cheerful voice broke into her thoughts. "Well, how was dinner?"

Hayley sighed and forced a smile to match his. "Marvelous. Thanks so much." She slid her hand across Peter's arm to rest there. "And thanks for the story. It explains a lot I couldn't understand."

They moved apart as the waiter returned Peter's credit card and receipt. Peter signed the slip and escorted Hayley out to the car. They drove through the city in silence, and Peter pulled onto the Boulevard of the Allies toward Oakland.

"Hayley?" Peter asked.

"Yes?" She leaned back in the cushion of the seat and turned her head toward him. In the dim light she could see Peter's solemn profile, so unlike him, but an expression, she'd discovered tonight, that was very much a part of him.

"Be careful with David."

"Careful? I don't think I—"

"He has a tendency to hurt the people closest to him."

With sudden awareness, Hayley knew that Peter must sense some of her attraction for David. Or perhaps Peter meant *close* in the working sense. Hayley appreciated the warning. Having seen some of David's terrible anger and knowing how protective he was about the company, Hayley was sure she wanted to avoid contact with him. He was her boss, after all. A great peace settled on her. She should have reminded herself of that fact long ago and with a lot more conviction.

"I don't have any intention of getting that close to him," she said firmly.

Beside her, Peter's shoulders relaxed, and he let a breath whistle through his teeth. "Just checking."

Hayley laid a light hand on his sleeve. "Sounds like you're protecting your interests."

Peter grinned and threw a glance her way. "And how are my interests tonight?"

"Very solid," Hayley assured him.

CHAPTER 6

When Haley had told Peter that she intended to keep her distance from David Mansfield, she had not reckoned on proposal writing. Given that Hayley understood how the whole information operation would fit together, the writing and the discussions revolved around her. After meetings with team members ended, Hayley would head for David's office to review points and ask questions, while he guided, advised, and prodded when needed.

Hayley and David usually sat on opposite sides of his conference table with papers spread out in front of them. The table provided a physical barrier between them, but David's masculine attractiveness continued to tug at Hayley. As the plan for the center grew, so did her admiration and understanding for her boss. Respecting him in a professional sense only increased her desire to know him better, to feel his arms around her. She left the late-afternoon sessions drained from the contradictory forces of reason and emotion pulling her.

If she had to contend only with the daily review sessions, Hayley believed she could have sustained her promise to Peter and to herself. To Hayley's chagrin, David himself wrecked her shaky peace. He'd called to share a rumor about a competitor and dropped into her office to give her drafts. It seemed whenever Hayley looked up from her work, David's broad back and brown hair were bent over the old clippings and photo files. His sudden appearances no longer flustered her, but her wariness increased. The more she saw of David, the more she wanted to know. After two weeks, Hayley feared she was losing ground with her reason while her emotions were strung taut.

While planning on the proposal continued, so did the routine work of the library, and Hayley realized that to maintain both tasks would require extra effort. She resigned herself to an after-hours search to find fax machine prices. Hoping to verify printed prices with those online, Hayley first scanned the extra collection of equipment catalogs shelved in the storeroom. Stacking the most useful catalogs in a pile, Hayley surrounded them with her arms and headed back to the library.

As she approached the glass double doors, Hayley noticed that the overhead lights were on. For a moment, the sight stopped her, since she knew she had shut the lights out after Maggie had left. She proceeded cautiously and was surprised to see David, engrossed in reading papers at one of the tables. As the door swung shut behind Hayley, his head jerked up.

"There you are," David stated. "Maggie said you were staying. Can't get enough of the place, can you?"

"Hardly that," Hayley replied with sarcasm. She gestured to the pile in her arms with a jerk of her head. "I wanted some quiet to look over equipment catalogs. What's your excuse?" Tired and irritated that she would have to deal with David at close quarters, Hayley flung the last at him like a challenge.

David's eyebrows lifted a fraction before he answered. "Just trying to write a proposal. Any complaints?"

Hayley felt like crawling under a rock. She smiled sheepishly. "None. You're the boss. You go ahead and do whatever you like." She turned and walked into her office where she dropped the catalogs onto her chair.

Before Hayley straightened, David was behind her, standing in the doorway. She turned to face him, and he threw her such a tender look that for a moment the proposal, the office, and the world melted away.

Almost in a trance, she took a step toward him. Abruptly, the spell broke.

"I'm having trouble with a section of the proposal over here," David said in a businesslike tone. "Do you have a few minutes to help me out?" A shudder of disappointment ran down Hayley's back. He walked out into the library and picked up a sheet from the pile. "Does this sound right to you?"

Hayley congratulated herself on taking the sheet without dropping it. After a second, she shook her head and read it again, finally with the concentration she knew she needed. She wondered who had written this paragraph. It was terrible. She glanced at David who sat quietly waiting for her answer. If he had written this... *I hate editing,* she thought furiously. *Someone's ego always gets stepped on. I don't want to be the one to tell him—*

Hayley rubbed the back of her neck.

"That bad, huh?" David said.

She glanced at him then studied the page again. "It's salvageable. From what I heard at the Industry Day, the review committee will be looking for more detail, less jargon and rhetoric. I'd rewrite it."

He held out a red pencil. "Please do."

She swallowed her relief at David's calm. She took the pencil and began to mark the paper, speaking while she did. "I'd put this sentence first, then take out this whole paragraph and substitute another example." She scribbled and talked until the page was covered with red pencil. Looking at her handiwork, she paused. "I hope you didn't want to use this page as it was."

David gave a tired chuckle. Hayley's stomach lurched at the sound. He didn't laugh often, but when he did, it was a pleasant sound that came from the heart.

"It's much better this way, red pencil and all. I've got another section here that's bothering me." He shuffled through the papers, found the sheet, and handed it to her.

She hesitated as she remembered the abandoned equipment catalogs and the cookies she was going to bake.

David's voice hardened. "Or do you have a date?"

"Date?" echoed Hayley. "Sure. If you consider wrestling with a bowl of cookie dough a date."

An embarrassed shadow stole into David's eyes. "What kind of cookies?"

"Chocolate chip, the only kind I make."

David set the sheet back down on the table. "I couldn't keep you away from the cookies," he said lightly.

It was a challenge and a choice. What kind of a choice was it, when the boss was asking the question? Anyway, she wanted to stay, to lift some of the burden of the proposal off his broad shoulders. The catalogs and the cookies could wait.

"You'd like to get this done, wouldn't you?" she asked, unwilling to be too eager.

"Yes."

"Then let's get started."

Obviously relieved, David drew a chair out for her, and they returned to the sheet of paper. Page by page, sentence by sentence, heads together, shoulders often touching, they reviewed sections of the manuscript.

Hayley cut words, added others, threw out whole pages, and made notes to get more information. David ceased to be her boss, an unreachable director who slipped in and out of everyone's work life. He was a colleague, asking for help, never hinting that he held power over her by virtue of his position.

Hayley learned quickly that although he was very good with the details of operating the company, David had difficulty presenting those details in terminology understandable to the uninitiated. For a man who seemed to have most areas of his business under control, David's lack of skill in report writing made him more accessible. Hayley enjoyed discovering this other side of David Mansfield, and she wondered when she would have more time to find other, more pleasant traits.

With a mental jerk, she halted that train of thought. What had Peter said about getting too close? What had she told herself about getting in too deep? David's tender look held a thrill as potent as fireworks on the Fourth of July. Sharing his work was as stimulating as a dive into a cold stream. Hayley sighed.

The sigh caught David's attention, and he stopped in midsentence to study her. She met his eyes, and he said bluntly, "Why didn't you say something? We've been at this for nearly two hours, and you haven't had dinner. Let's stop here and get something to eat."

Undecided, Hayley said, "I can get something at home."

"Aren't you hungry now? It'll take at least thirty minutes for you to get home."

"Yes, famished, but..."

"That settles it. And I'll pay."

The boss was back in command. But Hayley could not tolerate being bullied. "I don't need you to pay. I'd rather go home."

David gave her a furious glance, then threw his briefcase open, and began tossing papers into it. "I'm trying to thank you for the extra time you put in tonight, not seduce you."

They were both tired and hungry. Hayley could see that she was being too sensitive. Peter had said to be careful, and she was being careful. So how could dinner hurt? She watched as David jerked the jacket onto his shoulders. She made a decision.

"Dinner sounds marvelous," she said, hoping to still the agitated motion that disturbed her more than she would admit. "Where are you taking me?"

He slapped the case shut and turned to her. "Are you sure?"

Hayley's regret at her first reaction permitted only a nod.

"I know a little place down on Smithfield. I don't think it has a name, but they serve a wicked hamburger."

To Hayley's dismay, he had withdrawn again, and she blamed herself. She held out her hand. "Truce?"

David regarded her hand for a second then took it. "Truce."

Electricity sizzled up Hayley's arm and down her back. She shivered. Something must have happened to him, too, because he was now staring at her with eyes as deep as the ocean. Slowly, he drew her toward him. When Hayley was just inches from him, David dropped her hand and replaced the sudden loss of warmth with the heat of both his hands on her shoulders. She knew the kiss was coming. Her heart told her to be careful, but the doubts vanished under the touch of his lips. David enclosed her in a hug, moving his hands slowly over her back and through her hair. Just when Hayley thought she would faint from happiness, he pulled away.

He cupped her chin with one hand and studied her face as if trying to see into the core of her being. "What is it about you?" he whispered.

Still under the spell of the kiss, Hayley swayed toward him, tilting her head so that her lips invited his. David responded, but only with a brush of a kiss. "This is not the time or the place," he said gently. "Anyway, I'm hungry."

Hayley accepted his movement away from her. "I am, too," she said, thinking maybe, just maybe, it would be all right. With a smile, she turned her attention to the stack of papers and carried it to the office to lock in the file cabinet.

As she came out, David pulled the briefcase off the table. "Ready?" he asked.

"Ready."

The restaurant David had chosen was no more than an oversized hallway with a row of wooden tables along each wall. Chipped glass vases held dingy fabric flowers of unknown variety, and the bare tabletops were worn smooth and shiny.

"What's your pleasure?" David said, pointing to the blackboard that carried the day's fare.

"The mushroom burger, I think."

"Good choice. Anything to drink?"

"Iced tea."

He nodded and stepped to the bar, where their order was taken.

"They'll bring it to the table," he said as he sat down again and passed a glass of tea.

Silence descended. It seemed that weariness, excitement, and hunger had wrung the energy from both of them. Hayley's eyes drifted over the lack of decor. Her eyes focused on a tired-looking woman with enormous brown eyes sitting near the opposite wall with a dark, commanding man in a suit. She started when she realized that she was staring at herself. The entire wall was a mirror.

"Disconcerting, isn't it?" David said.

"Yes. Especially when I can see that I look as tired as I feel."

"I wouldn't expect anything less than exhaustion after fighting with the words from most of Mansfield's best minds. Thanks again. Before you came, I wasn't getting anywhere."

Hayley flushed. "I try my best."

David fingered his glass, and Hayley recalled his touch against her cheek and the warmth of his gaze.

David broke into her recollection. "You have some talent for putting words on paper. Ever write anything?"

"No. Just helped my father with his work."

"And your father is...?"

"Professor Albert Lancaster, Department of Sociology, Edinboro University."

David leaned back in the chair, his face full of remembrance. "Edinboro. That's beautiful country up there. I went up to Conneaut Lake for a weekend once. I was impressed."

"My family rents a cabin every summer at the lake."

"So that's what people with no ocean do," David said.

Hayley's eyebrows rose in question.

"My family usually goes to the shore on summer weekends. The Maryland shore, that is. I'm from Delaware."

Hayley smiled. "I've never met anyone from Delaware."

David groaned. "Everyone says that. I've even had people ask me if Delaware is in the United States."

"Well, is it?"

For a second, David stared at her in what seemed like stunned silence. She held on to her serious expression as long as she could, then giggled. David's entire face melted into a grin, then a laugh rolled out of his chest. When the waitress came to lay their plates in front of them, she saw two grown adults, hysterical with laughter.

"Two mushroom burgers?" she asked between chomps on a large wad of gum.

David gained control first and swallowed his next laugh. "Yes. Right here. Thank you."

The plates clattered to the table, and the bemused waitress returned to the kitchen, shaking her head.

Hayley sobered only with the greatest effort. "I can tell I'm exhausted. It wasn't *that* funny."

They exchanged a smile then attacked the food. Cheese and mushrooms dripped from the sandwiches, and they found little to say between diving for the napkins in the dull metal holder and managing the thick sandwiches.

Hayley popped the last bit of bun into her mouth and leaned back. "Done!"

"Did you enjoy it?" David asked.

"Absolutely. That was worth all the work tonight. Thanks."

"You're quite welcome." He pulled out a brushed leather wallet and dropped some bills on the table. "Ready?"

"Yes."

Back on the street, they walked in the humid evening air toward the building garage.

"Can I give you a lift home?" David asked.

"I can catch the bus."

"You're not considering riding the bus all the way to Oakland by yourself, are you?"

"I won't be by myself. The bus driver will be there."

David grunted. "A lot of good he would do you if you got mugged. He'd probably look the other way. Come on. I'll take you home."

"David!"

He took her arm. "No arguments. You'll be safer with me."

"Are you sure?" She was teasing, but in the darkness, she knew he could not read her expression.

His hand dropped away as if her arm were hot, and he backed a step from her. "Perhaps you're right," he said steadily. "I can't seem to be with you without making a pass. Good night." He swung from her and strode away.

"David, wait!" she called, but he did not stop. *What brought that on?* she wondered. Suddenly it was very important that there be no misunderstanding between them, no matter how small. She hurried after him, catching sight of him at the garage elevator.

"David."

He turned. In the harsh light she could see lines of — was that hurt? — across his face. He was turning away again.

"David, please. We have to talk."

The elevator door closed just as Hayley came up behind him. She touched him on the sleeve then reached out and drew her hand down his cheek, trying to smooth the weariness from his expression. "Don't you know that everything you've done, I've wanted, too? I was teasing back there."

David let out a relieved breath. "Then you don't feel pressured?"

The question caught her off guard. "Pressured?"

"I *am* your boss."

Hayley could have wept with relief. She had been worried that he might not want to get involved with an employee, and *he* was worried that she might feel compelled to respond to his advances because of his position! It was going to be all right.

"No, I don't feel pressured," she said quietly.

"Can I drive you home?"

"Yes, of course."

The elevator door slid open again. With a sweep of his arm, David guided Hayley in and kept his arm around her all the way to the blue sedan.

The ride in the car was as quiet as the ride in the elevator had been. David seemed lost in thought and roused himself only to ask directions to her apartment. With the events of the day and evening behind her, Hayley was glad to let the silence and the night surround them. The car was like a cocoon, dark and warm. And she did feel safe. Completely at ease. And tired — so tired.

The next thing Hayley knew, David was shaking her gently. "We're here. If you don't wake up, I'll be tempted to carry you in."

That brought her straight up in the seat. "No, that's all right. I'm awake now — I can manage." She gathered up her belongings, checking twice to be sure she had everything.

When she met his eyes to thank him, David was studying her intently, as if trying to find something he had glimpsed, but was now gone. As she sat mesmerized by his eyes, shining in the street lamp, he reached up and stroked her hair. The kiss that followed his touch was that of a friend, light and fleeting. "I'd better come with you," David said as Hayley stepped from the car. As he joined her, he added, "After the trouble I had getting you to accept the ride, I wouldn't want you to get mugged outside your apartment."

Hayley started to protest, but David's arm was on her elbow, steering her up to the second floor. Somehow, she fumbled with the key and let herself in. David hesitated at the door. For a moment, Hayley wondered if he wanted an invitation in. She was formulating how to tell him politely to leave when he said, "Everything all right?"

Finally understanding his hesitation, she looked around the room, walked to the bedroom, and flicked on the lights. Everything was as she had left it.

"Yes, fine."

"Then, good night." He shut the door behind him.

Hayley's hand drifted to her hair where David had touched her. Deep inside a low chord of contentment swelled and burst into a series of soft notes.

CHAPTER 7

The next morning Hayley leaped out of bed to marvel at the bright sunshine. In the shower, water beat on her with delightful patterns, and she crunched her cornflakes with gusto. The previous evening had revealed the human side of David Mansfield, and his actions had suggested that he was as attracted to her as she was to him. She hummed along with the radio, skipped a little on the way to the bus stop, and viewed the buildings around her with renewed interest.

True, she knew no more about the rift between David and Peter than she had before, and Peter's story still bothered her. But this morning she was certain that David could not have acted without good reason. Hayley now thought she could question him about that period in his life. His marriage to Julia had affected him deeply, and without knowing what had happened, Hayley was convinced she would never understand him. And understanding Joshua David Mansfield was becoming an obsession.

With reason, then, Hayley was delighted when David strolled into the library, glanced furtively around, and asked her for a date.

"The Tamburitzans are performing Saturday night at the Power Center. Would you like to go?"

The pleasure in her eyes was reflected in his as she said simply, "Yes."

"I'll pick you up around 7:15, and perhaps after the show we can go somewhere for a drink."

"That would be fine," Hayley answered and was pleased to see a glowing light build in his eyes.

At the same time, they both sensed a third presence in the library. David turned, and Hayley saw Maggie walking toward her office.

Maggie stopped when she recognized David and asked, "Did you get everything you needed?"

David smiled and nodded. "I got everything I came for." He gave Hayley a fiery glance, then threw a "See you later" over his shoulder as he departed.

Maggie continued to her office, and Hayley returned to her job of processing the latest new books.

A moment later Maggie leaned against Hayley's door. "How's the proposal coming? It must be all right if you have time to get back to the boring stuff."

"My part is completed," Hayley agreed, "and David is doing the final edit. He'll let us know if he needs anything. We have until next Friday, but I assume there'll be some overtime next week."

"Are you locking everything up?"

Hayley thought a moment then answered, "Well, not during the day when I'm working. But I do lock everything up at night. That's all right, isn't it?"

"That's fine. At any rate," Maggie added with a gesture toward Hayley's desk, "I don't think anyone could find anything on your desk if they tried. How do you do it?"

Hayley looked over the ruffled piles of paper that effectively covered the desktop and shrugged. "Organized disorganization. I know where everything is."

Maggie laughed. "Well, that's what counts."

The hours couldn't fly fast enough to Saturday evening. Hayley hoped an opportunity would arise to talk with David about Peter and Julia. Perhaps she would have the truth at last.

For the evening, she chose a soft, periwinkle-blue wool sheath. With her beige raincoat, the dress would be warm enough if the spring air turned chill. She also knew that the simple lines of the dress were flattering to her figure, and the color deepened her eyes to a dark chocolate. A string of pearls added just the touch of elegance needed for a late night drink. When she opened the door at David's knock and saw the blatant admiration in his eyes, her stomach unwound. It *was* going to be all right.

The blue sedan, which had been the scene of previous conversations, surrounded them with comfortable privacy, and they talked of small things. Hayley asked once about the proposal, and David firmly refused to discuss it. It seemed he was determined to make the evening as pleasurable as possible. Hayley gladly concurred.

Having lived in Pittsburgh for over two years, Hayley had heard about the dance troupe called the Tamburitzans but had never found time to see them perform. For over seventy-five years, students selected for their performing talents from Duquesne University and other schools, had reproduced the dances of Eastern Europe in what had become the longest running live stage show in the country. Tonight their performance presented the full range of the troupe's capabilities from the stately court polonaise danced in a slow three-quarter time to the rousing, foot-stomping mazurkas. The costumes blazed with color and light from rippling floral and striped fabrics and sparkling beaded vests. By the end of the evening, the audience clapped in time to the polkas and swayed to the haunting love songs. Hayley thrilled to see that David often joined in.

He was still humming later in the car, making a resonant sound that soothed Hayley.

"It sounds like you enjoyed yourself." she commented with a laugh in her voice.

"Immensely," David answered as he maneuvered the car out of the parking lot. "The group seemed to be *on* tonight."

"You've seen them before, then?"

"Every year since my marriage. My wife's nephew was a member of the group, so we went often. After he graduated, I continued to attend their shows." Although Hayley could not see David's face, she could hear the frown in his voice at the mention of his marriage and his wife. After an awkward pause, David continued, "I like to see young people preserving their cultural heritage."

"So your wife's family was Polish?" Hayley asked, trying to learn more about Julia.

"Czech." The silence lengthened. Finally, David threw a glance Hayley's way and said, "You know how she died." The statement could have been an accusation or a question.

Hayley hesitated, not knowing how to answer him without incurring that temper that seemed to appear at the mention of Peter or Julia. Into the pause, David said sarcastically, "Details care of my *good* friend, Peter Jameson."

"Yes, your good friend," Hayley countered, suddenly angry at the feud between the two most important men in her life. "Friend enough to worry about you even if you can't be civil to him."

"Was he worried when he seduced my wife?" David asked in a tone all the more threatening for its quiet certainty.

"You really believe that, don't you?" Hayley said in amazement. "You really believe that Peter, who thinks of you as a brother, would deliberately set out to hurt you."

"And what do you know about it?" David flared back. "What kind of trash did Peter tell you? That he was a victim? That Julia threw herself at him? Oh, no. It will take more than his word to convince me that he was not a full participant."

Hayley answered very softly. "Five years ago, you would have taken his word."

They were in Oakland again. Fifth Avenue reflected the nightlife of a college campus — flashing neon, pizza joints, corner pubs. A Jaguar roared out of a parking space in front of them, and David swung the car into the spot with restrained savagery. He shut off the lights and the engine then placed his hands on his knees before looking toward Hayley.

"I need that drink. How about The Pit?" Although his eyes radiated his annoyance, David's voice was flat.

"Fine," Hayley answered. When David swung out of the door, Hayley released her breath and clutched her hands together tightly to stop their shaking. She had never dealt well with anger, and David's barely controlled fury gripped her soul.

Inside The Pit, Hayley was aware of dim lighting, a gleaming walnut bar surrounded by people, white marble tables, and the simmering man beside her. A table in a far corner opened up, and David led her there with a strong hand at her elbow.

Hayley had taken her first sip of brandy before David spoke again. He rotated the glass of whiskey and water so that the ice clinked rhythmically against the sides.

"I can see we'll have to lay some ground rules if we're going to survive our conversations." His tone was light, his anger hidden. "I'm sure you've realized that I don't care to talk about my wife. You've obviously heard enough to form an opinion — and one that's not complimentary to me, it seems." He drank then set the glass down.

"From what I know about you and about Peter, I wonder how you could have thrown away such a friendship," Hayley stated as calmly as her nerves would allow.

A flash of pain shot through David's eyes.

"Is that what you think?" David took another drink then captured her hands between his. "Then I do need to explain. I was not totally blind to my wife's shortcomings. I confronted Peter several times with her stories. That last time, when Julia boasted that she and Peter were lovers and intended to marry, a mutual friend confirmed it." David's eyes reflected all the pain that revelation had cost him. "The proof was there. I could have forgiven him for wanting her. She was so beautiful. What I could not forgive was that Peter did not come to me first. Above all, I expected honesty from him."

David released her hands and let them rest on the table while he leaned back into the chair. "Can you understand that?" he asked softly.

Hayley nodded. Yes, she understood only too well. In the end, even though David professed a deep love for Julia, it was his bond with Peter that had determined the outcome of their confrontation five years ago.

Hayley wished that there was a way to bridge the gap between them. But just as quickly, she realized that she could not be that bridge. Working for one man, involved with both, she would only push them farther apart. Hayley knew that soon she would have to choose between them. She sighed.

"Hayley," David said intensely, "what's between Peter and me is just that. Between us. I don't want you to feel as if you should do something about it." Hayley blushed as he echoed her thoughts. "I don't want my argument with Peter to come between you and me."

This last statement came as a surprise. Hayley's eyes shot to his and found a warm gaze drinking in her expression.

"I don't think it could," Hayley replied and realized that she meant it.

Relief swept over David's face. "Good." He motioned to a waiter then said, "Would you like something else? Something to munch on?" he added with a glance at her almost untouched glass of wine.

"Yes, munchies would be great."

The waiter recited the available offerings while Hayley and David tested his patience with a discussion of the merits of each possibility.

When they finally decided on one plate of raw vegetables and one of nachos with cheese, the waiter left shaking his head.

David chuckled. "I didn't know you had a sadistic streak in you. I thought I was the only one who likes to give waiters a hard time."

"I learned from my brothers. Waiters were their favorite targets since they all had worked in restaurants. They were very good to waitresses, I recall."

"Sexist."

Hayley smiled, enjoying this light banter. "Without a doubt. But the waitresses appreciated it."

The sounds of a guitar and piano floated to their corner, and Hayley looked around. She saw a small dance floor topped by a stage just large enough for the two people now performing. The duo had started the set with a popular love ballad whose words spoke of hurting and forgiving.

David extended his hand. "Shall we dance?"

They walked to the dance floor, and David drew her close. In her dreams as a child, Hayley had often conjured up the image of a prince and princess floating around a ballroom, dancing a romantic waltz and oblivious to the people around them. The princess had always looked remarkably like Hayley, and excitement and fulfillment had quickened her senses. She had often thought that love must feel like that dream. As David led her though the dance, reality replaced the dream. There was no waltz. Instead of gold epaulets, the prince wore a dark blue suit that matched his eyes. But the sense of fulfillment could not be denied. David shifted closer to her, and she sighed in contentment. The music drifted off into a final chord, and David drew back yet kept her in the circle of his arms.

"Hayley," he whispered, caressing her with his eyes. "What are you doing to me?"

"I don't know what you mean." She realized that he was questioning his attraction for her, but she could not understand why he needed to question.

Then, as if trying to find the answer, David kissed her. The touch of lips to hers was a quiet searching of the special bond growing between them. Hayley's heart glided on air.

David slipped his arm around her shoulder and hugged her close while they walked back to the table. "I don't think I care." He answered his own question. "Tonight, I just want to enjoy it."

The rest of the evening they sat side by side, hands entwined, talking about life and work. First, there were teasing remarks while they ate dripping cheese on crisp nachos, then serious discussions when the food and drinks lay between them, forgotten in the urgency to know more about one another.

"So how do you like the job so far?" David asked after ordering another round of drinks.

Hayley smiled and shook her head. "That's a loaded question, you know. If I say I like it, you'll wonder if I'm playing up to you. If I say I don't, you'll think I'm ungrateful."

David's eyes sparkled. "Whatever the answer, I know it will be the truth."

"Perhaps, but that doesn't make the answer any easier." David let out an exasperated sigh, and Hayley immediately took pity on him. "Seriously, I do like it. I've got so much more to learn. I never realized the number of databases used for online searching, and there's so much more about contracting that I need to pick up. I guess when I stop learning in a job, it's probably time to move on."

Suddenly, David swung the conversation into a different track.

"Have you seen Peter lately?" he asked.

Hayley was instantly alert and wished she had not had that last drink. The casualness of the question did not fool her. If David was asking about Peter, he had a definite reason.

"Last week", Hayley answered, stroking her glass with her fingertips.

"Did he tell you anything about the DEP proposal?"

At that Hayley laughed. "You're both so much alike, did you know that? Not twenty minutes into the conversation with Peter, he was asking the same sort of question."

David's body went still. "What did you say?"

Hayley's eyes widened in amazement. The feeling of déjà vu would have been funny, except for the mounting anger in David's expression.

"What did you expect me to say?" she asked, laughing a little with the hope that his face would soften. After a moment, she realized that he expected an answer, and a note of despair resounded in her stomach.

Hayley laid her hand over his and felt his attempt to withdraw. She curled her fingers around his and squeezed. "Please don't ruin a perfect evening by being childish. I told him nothing, and I refused to talk about the proposal."

"And what if he let something slip? Would you tell me.?"

There was so much wrapped up in those two questions. Friendship weighed against company responsibility. To which man did she feel the stronger obligation?

She shook her head sadly and drew away from him. "You can't seriously think that Peter would slip anything in front of me. He knows I work for you, and he's too good at this game to be stupid." David's eyes still held their coldness. "I will not be used for this… sport of yours, David," Hayley said, wrapping both her hands around the glass and locking her eyes to his. "You said you did not want Peter to come between us."

David reached to pry her hands from the glass. "I would not use you. Ever. Forgive me." Then his hands dropped, and he took a long sip of his drink. "I've been competing with Peter too long."

"Competition can be positive if it's not taken to extremes."

David's smile answered her. "Thank you. I'll keep that in mind." He looked around the room and said, "If we keep this up, we'll be closing the place."

Hayley followed his gaze. The bar that had been so crowded hours before was nearly empty. The piano had long ago ceased its melodies, and the bartender washed glasses with a methodic swish of a towel while listening to a customer's low words.

"It's almost two. Shall I take you home?" David asked.

As before, David walked her to the door of her apartment. But this time, instead of waiting in the hall, he followed her into the living room to stand a few feet inside the door. When Hayley came back from checking the bedroom, David was waiting. Before she could react, he had covered the distance between them with two long strides and surrounded her with his arms. His lips found hers unerringly.

The power of the wine combined with the long, emotional talk drained Hayley's resistance. Waves of happiness rolled over her until her brain stopped processing each sensation and relinquished its hold on rational thought.

Then, abruptly, David pushed her away. His hand trembled as his fingers raked his hair. "Oh, Hayley," he said softly.

Hayley leaned toward him to recapture the warmth of his embrace.

David took her hand and kissed her palm. As his free hand stroked her hair, he said. "Go to bed now. I'll see you at the office." With a kiss to her forehead, he strode out, shutting the door behind him.

Hayley stood in the middle of the room, confused and angered by his sudden coolness. She hugged her arms around her waist as tightly as she could until the tears she was fighting fell slowly down her cheeks.

Then she drew the chain on the door and turned the dead bolt. She leaned against the door, wishing she could lock her heart's response as easily as she locked the door.

CHAPTER 8

He's avoiding me.

The thought struck Hayley as she read through the procedures section. There were only three days until the proposal was due. At a time when she and David should have been juggling the final details of the massive document together, she had spent the past day and a half watching the back of David's head as he walked out on her.

She sighed and dragged her attention back to the words. There it was again. The problem of the electronic conversion of the older, paper reports still had not been solved, and Pat hesitated to make any firm decision until David had considered all the alternatives.

"Well, J. David Mansfield," Hayley mumbled to herself, "whether you like it or not, you will have to stay in a room with me for more than two minutes, because I need an answer."

As she walked upstairs, she realized that the answer she needed had nothing to do with document conversion.

Why? Why is he avoiding me? Her mind ran through the possibilities. *He doesn't really like me. I'm too forward. He doesn't want to get involved.*

A smile grew on her face as that last thought crossed her mind. *He is involved.*

Hayley passed through the open door to the reception area and greeted Louise. "Is he in?" Hayley nodded toward the door.

"No, you just missed him," Louise said. "He went to the bank to talk about financing for some new project."

Hayley's smile collapsed, and she bravely tried to pin it back up.

From the desk, Louise said, "You needed to see him, I take it?"

Hayley dragged her eyes away from the closed door to David's office and turned back to Louise with a sigh. "Yes," she answered, waving Pat's written recommendations in the air. "It's about the DEP proposal and, without him, this section is dead in the water."

Hayley's gaze drifted to the door again with a wistfulness that only a blind person could miss. She felt rather than saw Louise's appraisal of her profile and silently chided herself for letting the personal aspect of her disappointment show through. She rummaged through her brain for a light conversational bridge out of the office, but as she faced Louise, the older woman said gently, "It's like a marriage, isn't it?"

"What is?" Hayley asked with a frown.

"Proposal writing. It's like a marriage. You spend a lot of hours with a very attractive, very competent man. You see him when he's tired, optimistic, discouraged, edgy. You argue. You work. You plan. You laugh a little. He takes you out once or twice."

As Louise talked, she described the events that had marked Hayley's relationship with David since the day work began on the proposal.

Hayley found her voice. "We couldn't get much closer."

"Except that you go home at night. Even though you spend more time with him than with any other person on this earth, when the work is completed, you go home. And when this proposal is finally finished, the circumstances will return to normal."

The word *normal* bounced through Hayley's mind like a tennis ball. Had her relationship with David ever been normal? Was it normal to lose control of her emotions every time he walked into the room? Hayley forced her mind to stop harping on her emotional reactions and focus on what Louise was saying in her motherly, nonjudgmental way. If Louise was trying to tell her that the electricity between David and her was a product of circumstances, Hayley couldn't believe it.

"I think we have something very special," Hayley ventured.

"Oh, I'm not saying you don't," Louise said with some relief in her voice. "You should bless your stars that you do, or this proposal would never have gotten done. And I'm not saying he doesn't care for you. He cares about everyone who works for him. A good working relationship *is* special..."

"Louise!" Hayley broke in.

Louise smiled ruefully at Hayley's expression and continued with less enthusiasm. "He does see women outside work. He works closely with women on the job. I have seen this type of thing happen before, and I don't want you to be hurt." Louise paused then smiled broadly. "I know what effect David can have on women. If I wasn't married to the most wonderful man in the world, I'd throw my hat in the ring." Hayley answered the smile with one of her own, and Louise added, "Just be careful."

In her mind, Hayley replayed all her encounters with David. True, there was an element of gratefulness in his attitude. She had rescued him from an unpleasant writing task. Even now, he might not be avoiding her, only showing the extent of his interest, employer to employee. In reflection, Hayley could understand Louise's concern. Louise was watching the situation from the outside, and to her, David's interest might look like previous encounters. The thought that David had made the same moves with another woman stabbed Hayley with jealousy, but that swiftly disappeared when Louise broke the silence.

"Now that I've thoroughly meddled, you can give me a good scolding."

Hayley shook her head. "No, you don't deserve that. I know what you're trying to say. I appreciate it."

"Then you're not angry with me?"

Hayley met Louise's worried gaze and realized that Louise had misinterpreted her silence. Hayley smiled. "Of course not. I'm glad you told me. I could be more objective."

Louise relaxed in her chair. "I don't want to see you hurt, that's all." Hayley nodded and made her way back to the library.

David returned that afternoon in a nasty mood. The meeting at the bank had not gone well. With the DEP proposal due on Friday and full sections of the technical volume waiting for editing, David considered his absence a waste and vented his frustration on his employees. Soon each member of the proposal team could relate a tale of lost tempers and unreasonable demands in addition to the usual apologies and quiet laughter.

Remembering Louise's words, Hayley kept her distance from David. In doing so, she had been the only one on the team who had not had a boisterous confrontation with him, and she prayed that state of affairs would last until Friday at three, when the proposal would be out of the office, and nothing more could be done about it.

In deference to Hayley's more fluid writing style, David dumped a printed copy of the manpower volume on her desk Wednesday evening and barked, "See that this gets proofed!"

Confronted with nearly six inches of paper, Hayley appealed to Louise.

"I know, I know," Louise commiserated. "We're not helping the trees with all that paper. Thank heavens for recycling. At least the tables and charts aren't here. David always does the final proof of the text in print. It's amazing the errors you notice once you get the text off the screen."

While Hayley read at the conference table in David's office, Louise made changes to the electronic master copy and ran automatic spelling checks. David popped in and out of the room, adding final touches, answering questions and scowling.

They worked until two a.m. that night and moved to the technical volume; they finished nearly the same time on Thursday. Both nights David drove Hayley home in detached silence. Hayley had recognized that his quiet moments were the most dangerous and sat as close to her door as possible so as not to break into his contemplation.

By late Friday morning, Hayley was exhausted. She positioned herself at the large graphics drawing board sticking small labels onto a paper floor plan. This was her own fault, Hayley reminded herself. She had asked for the extra plan, and Grant, one of the artists with a tendency to go *old school*, had drawn it nearly freehand, explaining it would be much faster than using the architecture software. But she'd have to place the labels.

Old school. Right. She'd remember next time not to ask Grant for last minute work.

It was slow going. The tiny labels kept slipping off the tip of the thin art blade she was using to place them. She willed herself to stay in control of her shaking fingers. By three o'clock this stupid proposal would be done, and then she could sleep. If she didn't deserve a long weekend now, she didn't know when she ever would.

The door swung open behind her. David appeared at her side.

"Are you done yet?" he demanded.

Steady, she told herself. *Keep cool.* "Just one more label, then it's ready to shoot and reduce," she answered through clenched teeth.

"You should have had Grant do that." His tone was still belligerent.

The control she had mustered slipped. "Grant has been here the last four nights getting those charts done for you, and he was here most of last night finishing the main floor plan. Putting labels on this was the least I could do. He looked like death warmed over this morning."

David's voice rose a fraction. "You don't look so wonderful yourself. You've put in just as many hours as Grant. It's asinine to let Grant walk all over you with his poor-old-man routine. This is his job, not yours."

In her haze of tiredness, Hayley took offense at the first thing he said. "How do you expect me to look when I've had exactly ten hours of sleep in the past three nights? On top of that, I've had to put up with your foul moods. You've growled and fumed and yelled all week, even though every person here has pushed himself to the limit for this proposal." By this time, she was waving the pointed tip of the knife in his face so that he took a step back out of its reach. "You haven't got an ounce of gratitude for all the work they've done. Well, *I* appreciate how much effort went into this floor plan."

"So you don't think I appreciate all the work?" he said, a dangerous gleam in his eyes. He stepped closer so that his face was inches from Hayley, forcing her to strain her neck to meet his eyes. "I have plenty of gratitude," he whispered and caught her chin between his fingers. His other hand clamped the hand holding the knife to the table. Then, as if he felt secure from the knife, his lips deliberately lowered to hers.

At first she was too stunned to react, but then the pressure of his hand against the knife reminded her of where they were — in the bright graphics room with the door half open and curtains drawn back from the glass walls for anyone to see. With her free hand, she pushed against his chest, but the hand under her chin made retreat impossible.

The kiss ceased. Hayley's lips tingled.

With a smile, David said, "You see, I do appreciate you."

Hayley felt the color fly into her face. He was laughing at her, using what he knew to be her weakness. It was a game to him, just as

Louise had warned. In a burst of fury, Hayley's open hand shot out. The slap echoed like a cannon blast in the room.

She watched in fascination as a red mark in the pattern of her hand slowly grew on his cheek. There were slow, pounding seconds of silence during which David's eyes hardened to stone. "That better be ready," he snapped and strode from the room.

Hayley looked down at her hands. They were trembling, and her right hand smarted. She clasped them together then turned with a decisive movement to finish placing the last label.

The label slipped from the knife twice, and twice she urged the thin piece of sticky film on to the floor plan and tried to reposition it. The third time, the knife flipped out of her fingers and fell to the floor, taking the film with it. She stared at the knife rolling smoothly toward the corner of the room, dropped her head in her hands, and cried.

At three o'clock in the afternoon, the whole of Mansfield Inc. breathed a collective sigh of relief. The courier had arrived to convey two paper copies of the completed proposal to the government's contracting officers. Louise had verified that the web portal created for electronic access to the proposal contents was *live*. Now the company could get back to business as usual while waiting for the decision. Immediately after the courier toted the boxes out on a small hand truck, Hayley picked up her purse and coat and went home. Within fifteen minutes of entering her apartment, she had shed her skirt and blouse, pulled on a long nightgown, and dropped into bed.

She slept straight through to Saturday and woke only as the morning was changing into afternoon. She spent all of Saturday curled on the couch with a book, but admitted by evening that she had made little progress. Although her eyes scanned the words on the page, her mind was in the graphics room watching David Mansfield's face freeze into indifference after her outburst.

I should have had more control, Hayley berated herself. *But he was entitled to that slap. He acted just like Louise said. I was a fool not to see it.*

On the other hand, Hayley continued her musing, *slapping your boss is not an action designed to gain favor. Especially when you wanted that kiss. Admit it, Hayley, you responded.*

No one she had ever met could arouse such fury and tenderness in her. Not Gary, the boy she dated in college; not the men she knew in graduate school. Not even Peter who loved her. Louise's words floated back to her. *"It's happened before."*

"And it's happened again," Hayley said aloud to the empty room.

She could lose her job for that slap. The thought shook her. So did the realization that she probably should quit her job and file sexual harassment charges because of the kiss.

Hayley lowered her head to the book in frustration. Her concentration soon wavered, and she saw David's face on the page, felt his lips on hers, his fingers firmly around her wrist, restraining yet not hurting. She threw the book aside and walked into the kitchen for a snack. She selected a pear from the refrigerator and paced to the living-room window. From here, she could view the tall buildings on Forbes Avenue and, above her, a hazy sky.

In slapping him, she had been slapping herself, she thought. Trying to punish him for her own gullibility, for her response to him. She relived the long hours they had spent on the proposal. They'd argued over wording, then they had laughed over some phrasing that had turned silly in their fatigue.

"It's almost like a marriage, isn't it?"

As Hayley watched the sun slide behind the buildings, that phrase reverberated in her mind. Not only was it like a marriage, it was the marriage she wanted. An equal partnership in the work, the dreams, the troubles, the happiness of the man she loved.

There. She had admitted it. She said it again, this time aloud. "I love him."

The warnings had been for nothing. The sky darkened outside as Hayley let this realization settle into her being. She loved Joshua David Mansfield. A man who had difficulty trusting, but who held the power of exquisite delight over her. Her boss.

To the bright moon and twinkling stars, Hayley pleaded, *"Now* what do I do?"

CHAPTER 9

A sudden downward gust of wind jerked the kite toward the earth. Hayley tugged on the string. The kite floated toward her then popped into a rising airstream, taking its fluttering tail with it. She watched its progress and judged its balance as she maneuvered it among the shifting winds.

This creation pleased her. She had fashioned the kite from balsa wood and used the traditional crossed-stick design, but she had bowed the shorter stick to give the structure more stability. The spiral painted on the cloth body spun in uneven circles as the wind bounced the kite at whim. After half an hour, Hayley decided that she wanted to lengthen the tail and adjust the bow. Slowly she reeled the kite in until it landed gently about four feet in front of her.

As she made her adjustments, Hayley congratulated herself for making this Sunday outing to Schenley Park. If there was anything that could take her mind off her struggle with this new dilemma, it was launching a kite in breezy April weather. When she flew a kite, she was with it, floating along among the clouds, tied to reality by the merest thread.

If only I could avoid reality a little longer, she thought. Reality meant a pair of deep blue eyes that haunted her dreams and questions that she didn't know how to answer or even how to ask. Did David love her, or was his attraction a passing physical fancy as Louise had suggested? How could she want something permanent with a man who'd accused his best friend of seducing his wife? What would he do when he saw her again after the confrontation on Friday?

Her fingers retied the strings on the bow while her mind jumped from one question to another. A faint whirr from above interrupted her questioning, and she looked up. Standing a few yards from her,

David was holding a camera at eye-level. Even when he was casually attired in blue jeans topped by a plaid shirt and blue sweater, his taste and physique could not be denied.

David lowered the camera slowly. A lopsided grin appeared on his face. "Do you mind? The lighting is perfect. I couldn't resist."

To hide the sudden rush of pleasure and relief, Hayley merely shrugged and bent over her work. She heard the camera steadily whirr, pause, then whirr again. She prepared to launch the kite but sensed that David had stopped shooting. When she glanced his way, the camera hung around his neck, and he was watching her, his arms akimbo, the sleeves on his sweater and shirt pushed up to reveal his forearms. His attention made her nervous, but at least he wasn't angry.

"Are you just going to stand there, or do you want to help?" Hayley asked lightly, determined not to show her nervousness.

"I don't know what to do." His statement was one of fact, but Hayley took it as assent.

"Well, take off that hunk of technology, and I'll show you."

With no comment, David did just that. The camera disappeared into the soft leather bag on his shoulder, and the bag slid gently to the ground not far from where Hayley was standing. He straightened. "Now what?"

At that moment, it didn't matter that a load of unfinished business surrounded them. All Hayley could feel was her love for him, and a deep gratitude to higher beings that her behavior on Friday had not driven him away permanently.

Picking the kite off the ground, Hayley said, "You're going to help me launch this. Hold the kite at the bottom of the long stick. No, no, that's upside down." She turned the kite around so that the cross bar was nearer the top and placed his hand on the stick. Afraid to admit what this proximity was doing to her self-control, Hayley hurried on to the next instructions. "Now you stand over there, about ten yards that way. And face me." When he was in position, she said, "Hold the kite up a bit over your head. Can you feel the wind against it?"

"Yes."

"Can you feel the gusts?"

"Yes."

Hayley reeled in the extra line until it was taut from her spool to the kite. "Okay. When you feel a gust, push the kite, toss it straight up — not too hard — and give a holler so I know you're going to let go." He was standing so still that Hayley wasn't sure he had heard. "Got that?"

"Aye, aye, Captain!" he said with a curt salute.

Hayley smiled and checked the line. "I'm ready. Any time."

She waited, her usual patience in this process dissolving into anxiousness. She pulled her mind away from the man, and the questions between them, concentrating instead on the kite.

David's shout just seconds later focused all her attention. The kite flew straight up, and Hayley felt the pull of the wind against the cloth. She kept the string taut while gradually letting more line out, allowing the perfect upward air current to carry the kite high into the blue.

"How'd I do?" David's voice came at her ear, and Hayley jumped.

"Fine." She watched the kite again then added. "It was perfect. That was just the right wind."

The right wind. A perfectly balanced kite in the air. The man she loved beside her. Hayley shivered with the enormity of the happiness around her.

"Cold?" David asked.

"It's flying," Hayley answered with a look his way. "That always makes me feel… well, happy. Carefree."

They watched the kite float almost motionless for several minutes.

David broke the silence. "I couldn't find you Friday afternoon."

Hayley glanced at his face. It was as noncommittal as the words were. "I went home early."

He nodded. "So Maggie said. I wanted to thank you for all your work. The proposal was the best I think this company has ever submitted, and a lot of the credit belongs to you."

Hayley let a short laugh escape while she tried in vain to conquer her blush. "Oh, I really didn't do that much…"

David nodded in agreement. "I guess, come to think of it, you didn't. You kept Grant's artistic temperament from getting in the way of those charts. You stayed up half the night with Louise proofing. You endured my foul temper… and my advances."

Hayley kept her eyes fastened to the flying kite. "I'm sorry—"

"I'm the one who should apologize. I deserved it. I had been wondering if anything could get through that professional shell you wrap around you. I found out."

Hayley's face burned with embarrassment. She blurted, "You should thank the others—"

"But I did. Friday afternoon. I called a meeting, had some wine and cheese sent in from the deli, and thanked everyone for the outstanding job. You see, Hayley," he added softly, "I do care."

Her attention swung from the kite to his face. She was lost. The words were for the company; his eyes were for her.

"I know," she whispered.

His arm slid around her shoulders, and she knew total security. He bent to press his lips to hers, and her heart raced faster than the wind. A voice in her whispered a warning. She pushed it away.

He pulled back too soon. He seemed to be a great distance away, watching her as if studying some marvelous formation of clouds in the sky, an odd, dazed look over his brow.

A strong, abnormal yank on the line forced Hayley's attention back to the kite.

"Oh, no!" she cried. The upper air had become turbulent, and the kite struggled for steadiness, bobbing and weaving like a boxer looking for his opening. The tail had ripped partway from its attachment and twirled wildly.

Without conscious thought, Hayley began to bring the injured kite back to earth. "Here, hold this!" She shoved the reel of line into David's hands, noticing his astonishment but ignoring it.

"What do I do with this?" he demanded.

"Just stand there," she called back. Already she had walked about ten yards from him, feeding the line through her fingers. The she began to walk backward slowly and steadily. "Wind up the slack," she called and felt the weight of the line lift as David wound it back onto the reel. When she had almost reached her drafted partner, she began the procedure again until the kite was floating directly above her head. She reached up and plucked it out of the air.

"I thought you were a goner," she whispered to the kite.

"What happened?" David asked from behind.

"The tail wasn't secure, see?" She showed him the loose staples. "And when the wind got stronger, the tail just pulled away and wasn't weighting the kite properly. If the tail had ripped off, the kite would have been uncontrollable. I might not have been able to get it down without a crash."

"You could have bought another."

"I didn't buy this. I made it. It takes several hours to put a kite together, and the balance of this one is particularly good. I don't like to see my work go to waste as kindling for a fireplace."

David handed her the reel. "Someday I'd like you to teach me how to make one."

She picked up her knapsack of tools. "I'd like that." She straightened to be confronted with his face close to hers. The breeze had blown waves of his hair over his forehead, and Hayley reached out to brush the locks back. She caught herself before completing the action.

David swung his camera case on his shoulder, "I'm starved. Know of any place open on Sunday afternoon? I'd offer to pay, but I'd rather not argue with you today."

His tone told Hayley he was joking, and she smiled with him at the shared memory. "We could have potluck in my apartment, if you don't mind surprises."

Relief flooded through Hayley when she saw the flash of laughter in his eyes. He was not going to fire her. He wasn't angry for the slap. The world was just fine.

"Surprises are what I live for," David said.

They walked to Hayley's apartment, and, on the way, she had a moment of panic. She had not straightened up before she'd left on the kite-flying expedition, and she had no idea if there was enough food in the house for dinner. In addition to the housekeeping problems, she asked herself several times what had possessed her to ask him over. Then she watched his handsome profile as he walked beside her, and she knew the answer.

The apartment's appearance lived up to her worst expectations, and while David was shifting his camera on to the chair and viewing the room with a slow, thoughtful look, Hayley scurried around, picking up pajamas and glasses.

"I didn't expect company," she said.

"I like it," David said, not at all perturbed. "It's homey and comfortable. Somehow I knew your place wouldn't be a sterile showcase."

"Too much work. I have other things to do." She offered her hand to him. "Let's check on dinner."

She led him to the alcove kitchen and left him leaning in the doorway while she searched the refrigerator. "How about... well, I don't know." She pulled open the crisper. "I have lettuce," she said with a question in her voice.

David joined her at the door and said, "I see a good-looking tomato beside me."

Hayley swung to him in astonishment. "That was terrible!"

His eyes danced with laughter. "It got your attention." Then his lips met hers in a heart-melting kiss. "I won't be slapped for that, will I?"

"Brute!" Hayley teased and kissed his cheek. She turned back to the refrigerator. "Here's a tomato and a few carrots. We can have salad." David took the vegetables from her and laid them on the counter by the sink.

Hayley continued her search in the freezer. "Frozen lemonade."

"I'll make that," David offered.

"Taking the easy part, I see." She tossed him the can. "Opener's on the hook above the sink. There's a pitcher on the right above the oven." She heard the bang of the cupboard door when she spied a box in the corner of the freezer. "I knew it was here. Boil-in-a-bag roast beef hash. OK?"

David was coaxing a lump of lemonade into the pitcher. "Sounds good."

Hayley found a pot, filled it with water and put it on the burner to heat. When she had set the gas flame, she said, "I'm not very hungry. Will that be enough?"

"Do you have any bread?"

"Hmm... half a loaf of Italian."

"Enough."

Hayley pulled the wrapped package from the refrigerator and set it on the stove to warm by the heat of the burner.

"I see you do lemonade well," she acknowledged the filled pitcher. "Can you handle salad while I set the table?"

"It's a tough job, but someone has to do it."

Hayley shook her head at his humor. She set out a bowl, a knife, and a cutting board. "You're on your own." Then she turned her attention to the table. While she found plates and napkins, she set out to learn more about the David Mansfield who existed beyond Mansfield Inc.

"Louise said you took those pictures in the conference room. They're very good."

"Thanks."

"I don't know much about photography, but I like them. Where did you learn?"

The click of the knife against the cutting board punctuated his words. "In college, from a photography professor who was delighted to show a computer jock the joys of art."

"A computer jock?"

"That was my major. Computer science. There's not much time left for liberal arts after all the programming I was required to do. I saw some of Dr. Kister's work in the student union and decided I wanted to learn something totally removed from computers. He taught me about perspective and lighting. Lent me a camera to start. I'm indebted to him," he finished on a quiet note.

"I think everyone needs an outlet like that," Hayley said, matching his tone. "Mine is making kites." A comfortable silence settled, then Hayley asked. "How did you do the one with the sunset over the house on the North Side?"

As David explained about time exposure, shutter speeds, and telephoto lenses, Hayley pulled the frozen bag of hash from the box and dropped it into the boiling water. With her attention focused on the impromptu lesson in photography, she miscalculated the angle of the bag above the water. The bag hit with a solid plop that spewed boiling water over her right hand. Pain shot through her fingers to her elbow. She cried out.

David's discourse stopped abruptly. "Hayley?"

"I just played bombs away with the hash, and it backfired." She managed a laugh but clutched her wrist and slowly moved her fingers. "It hurts," she whispered.

David was beside her, his face pale. He gently took the injured hand within his own. The palm was already turning red. He pulled her over to the sink, thrust the water on full to cold, tested it, then guided her hand under the water. Waves of relief flowed through her hand and all through her body as the stinging subsided.

"Keep it there," he ordered, and moved to the freezer. As he scooped ice cubes from the bin, he said roughly, "Do you have a towel?"

"On the side of the fridge."

He wrapped the cubes in the cloth then pushed Hayley into a chair. Gently, he laid the cloth in her hand and held it there. Finally, the cold conquered the searing heat, and Hayley's shoulders relaxed.

"Better?"

Hayley could finally forget the pain long enough to look into David's worried eyes. He was clearly as shaken as she.

"Much."

He knelt beside her for over ten minutes, pressing the ice on her hand. When he lifted the ice, the redness remained, but the pain was now a tolerable ache.

"Thanks," she whispered with a weak smile.

David bent and kissed the wounded palm. She gazed in wonder at the thick brown hair at the back of his head, and, with her free hand, she combed her fingers through the locks, reveling in the clean silkiness of it.

David rose and pulled her into his arms. He held her close, his desire to protect and cherish her communicated through the soft stroking of her hair.

"Hayley, Hayley," he whispered against her cheek, and her name had never sounded so beautiful.

The pain in her hand was a memory replaced by the sweet calm that now engulfed her. The world righted in his arms. Hayley was home, and she knew she never wanted to leave.

"Oh, David, I love you," she sighed.

He stiffened then drew back to look deeply into her eyes, his hands on her shoulders, holding her still. He backed up a few steps, his eyes never leaving her face. His expression, which before had been tender, was now blank.

"David?" Hayley scanned his face, his sudden withdrawal more frightening than any other mood she had seen.

He walked to the table and leaned on it, the muscles in his back bunched in tension.

"David?" Hayley said again and touched his shoulder.

He threw up his hand as if to ward her off, took a deep breath and said softly, "I'd better go."

With amazing speed, he retrieved his camera bag from the living room, strode to the door, and slammed it behind him.

CHAPTER 10

Hayley wrapped her arms around her waist and squeezed until her arms ached. Finally, she walked to the bathroom and splashed stinging cold water on her face. When she raised her head from the towel, a portrait of distress confronted her in the mirror. Her skin was chalk-white, and her eyes dark and upset. She rubbed the back of her neck and looked away from the strange, haunted woman in the mirror. When she looked again, the woman was still there. She hurried out of the unsympathetic light.

Now, half an hour after David Mansfield had rejected her declaration, reaction set in. The injured hand throbbed dully. She surveyed the kitchen and whispered, "Why?" to the salad and pot of water. Then she sank into a chair. Thoughts which had been impossible just minutes before overpowered her. Why had he left? What had she done to drive him away? Why did she have to love him so much?

In desperation, Hayley dialed David's apartment number, his mobile number, and then his private office number. At all three phones she heard an insistent ring, but no answer. She left messages and considered going to his place, but decided that if he wasn't answering his phone, he did not want to be disturbed.

She began to complete the dinner preparations, not because she was hungry, but because the movement kept her hands steady. When she got to the pot of water, a wave of anger rolled through her. *Who does he think he is? Wrangling an invitation to dinner then leaving without a word? What am I going to do with all this?*

She answered herself by locating plastic containers in a drawer and dumping salad and hash into their respective dishes. As she worked, she raged at herself. *What a fool you are! Everyone has told you what he's like. He has a girl for every project. He hurts his best friends. He doesn't let anyone close to him. Why did you ever think that you could be different?*

A feeling of loss swept over her, so deep that tears streamed unheeded down her cheeks. With a final gulp, Hayley straightened her shoulders. She had needed that cry. She pulled a kitchen towel from the plastic ring on the refrigerator and wiped her face.

Remember who you are, she thought, *and who he is. You're just an employee. A good one —* she sniffed and blew her nose *— but an employee nonetheless. Well, fine, Mr. Mansfield. Now I know where I stand.*

In complete selfishness, Hayley prayed Mansfield wouldn't win the DEP contract.

At eight-thirty the next morning, as Hayley stood at the file in her office pushing thick folders of DEP material into place, David entered the library. Hayley's heart lurched. She steeled her heart against his good looks and continued to work in the file until she heard the office door close with a quiet click.

"Good morning," David said quietly.

Hayley gave him a dismissive glance. She noted the dark smudges under his eyes and the line creasing his forehead. She wondered if she looked as bad, then decided he wouldn't care. "Good morning," she answered coldly and returned to the file.

"Hayley," he whispered, pleading.

She turned to him. His hands were hidden in his pockets, and his eyes burned with inner anguish.

"I'm sorry," David said. "I'm sorry I left the way I did yesterday." He ran a hand through his hair. "I didn't know what else to do."

"You could have talked to me," Hayley cried. "Told me what was wrong."

"How could I tell you when *I* don't know?" he lashed out then swung to face the library.

Stunned by this startling admission, Hayley said nothing.

Finally, David spoke distinctly to the glass. "For four years, I've worked to drag this business out of nothing. Escaping the past, ignoring the future except when it affected the company." He turned back to Hayley, a decision set in his face. "I'm not ready to take another risk."

Hayley thought she knew the reason. "Especially when I'm your employee. No need to explain."

David gaped at her in astonishment. Then his face melted into a look of love so tender that Hayley's heart leaped against her chest.

"No," he whispered and moved toward her, a rueful smirk playing on his lips. "That stopped being a consideration a long time ago." His fingers brushed a stray curl from her shoulder. "The truth is I don't have what it takes to be part of a couple. Look what happened the last time I tried."

Several seconds had flown before the essence of what he'd said reached Hayley's brain. He had not left yesterday because of her, but because of his own fear — the fear of failing again as he thought he had with Julia. How could he think that he alone was to blame?

"It takes two in any couple," Hayley said. "Surely you don't think the last time was all your fault."

"I know myself well enough to realize that my behavior and the outcome might not be any different with someone else."

"You hardly give yourself a chance. Every time we get close enough to make some progress, you run." She caught his hands in hers. "Don't give up on what might be," she urged. "There's something special happening here. I'd like to try."

"No."

Hayley shook with frustration. "You're condemning us both to pain because of something that might happen. I am not Julia. You are not the same person you were five years ago. You don't know the future."

"I do know that I will not let you shoulder my baggage."

Hayley was prepared to beg for a relationship so precious to her that disregarding it would be like disregarding an arm or a leg.

"David…"

"No." David cut her off and stepped out of her reach. "It's gone too far already."

Tears that Hayley had thought were long shed filled her eyes, and her throat ached with the struggle to hold them back. For her efforts, only one drop slid down her cheek. David moved, but she flinched and he retreated, resignation in every line of his body.

Hayley drew herself up to match his gaze. "What do you want?"

"I want a business relationship."

Hayley searched his face in vain for some wavering of his resolve. Perhaps in time she could show him that he could change. He cared about her. He might even love her. For now, she realized that he needed time and space. And she was the only one who could give it to him.

"All right." She nodded.

His sigh of relief stabbed sharply through Hayley. In her head, she knew she had done the right thing, but her heart cried for what could have been. As she watched, he turned on his heel and strode from the office.

Hayley survived Monday then focused on Tuesday. By Wednesday, she had stopped looking toward the library entrance every few minutes, and by Thursday, the ringing phone no longer jangled against her nerves. She thought she might be able to endure the separation David had thrust upon her. By Friday, she realized that if David continued to avoid her, she would never have the chance to rekindle their attraction. They could be living on separate planets.

The planets of the ninth and tenth floors orbited no closer during the following week. As Louise had predicted, things returned to normal. Hayley practiced online searching, helped Maggie with background for several proposals, and cataloged new books. After the flurry of the DEP writing, the pace seemed almost calm. No impossible deadlines, no emotional upheavals. Just the day-to-day pressures of a library operating in an inherently stressful environment.

After two weeks, Hayley was prepared to invade the higher territories just to make sure that the president was still in charge. She was making up a plausible excuse to go to the front office when Louise called.

"Meeting for the DEP proposal in fifteen minutes in the conference room up here. They're asking for the Best and Final."

Best and Final. Hayley took a deep breath. That meant the DEP had narrowed the field of bidders and was asking for each company's most economical offer for performance of the contract. To show that the company could provide the most value for the money.

Hayley slipped into the room right before Louise. The rest of the team was already there. As soon as they were seated, David began.

"I've got the section-by-section recommendations here. In each case, we're asked to pare down the cost as well as state changes that we think will make the operation more efficient. We have until next Friday. That's only a week away, so the timetable will be tight." He paused to glance around the table, his expression reflecting the gravity of the situation. "The rumor is out that PAJ is our competition, so we'd better be good."

Hayley groaned inwardly. Peter's company. She saw Dr. Matt and Jeff exchange significant glances. The talk was when PAJ and Mansfield went head to head, both would be out for blood.

David continued to make assignments. "I'll need rough ideas for the changes by tomorrow afternoon." At the collective groan, he smiled. "Yes, folks, that's Saturday. You're all on call this weekend. I'll start integrating material, and the document will be back to you on Tuesday. Then we'll see where we stand. I'll be doing the final edit myself, so make it legible, right, Jeff?"

Laughter rippled around the table. Jeff's handwriting was notorious.

Jeff blushed. "Everything through Louise, I promise."

"Good luck, Louise," Eileen said with feeling. Another round of laughter rose.

Hayley joined in halfheartedly. *He's going to do the edit alone*, she thought in pain. *He really does want to avoid me.*

"Well, people, next Friday will be upon us before we know it." David's cool voice dismissed the meeting.

The group straggled out, each member grumbling in his own way about the overtime and missed sleep.

As soon as they were out of earshot of the conference room, Louise turned to Hayley and said heatedly, "I can't believe it! Did you hear him? Do the final edit alone? Everyone knows you're the better writer. Whatever gave him the idea to do this himself?" Hayley shrugged to conceal the relief she felt at having her suspicion confirmed. He was willing to suffer through the worst part of the proposal just to stay away from her. "It's his choice, Louise."

"I know, but surely—" Louise broke off and slowed her pace down the hall. "Did something happen between you two?"

The soft question fell like a rock on Hayley's stomach. Was it that obvious? She attempted a light answer. "You'd do better to ask what didn't happen." She felt Louise's pointed stare and knew the color was rising in her face.

"Well, whatever the situation, he's a fool to stonewall you out of this writing. Men!" Louise added under her breath.

Hayley could have hugged her. Louise would not censure her and plague her with questions, just point out facts. Hayley had counted on the proposal rewrite to provide opportunities to plead her case with David. His announcement had routed those plans. In a way, she felt she had a reprieve. At least for a while longer she would not have to endure his watchful uneasiness.

Back at her office, Hayley read the suggested changes from the DEP and sighed. This might not be too bad. The contract officers wanted more trained librarians on staff. Easy enough to do with new résumés. They were also concerned with the turnaround time for online database searches. The proposed one week was too long; three days would be better. How was she going to cut the time to three days? Searching time alone could be that long if the question was complicated. They wanted the results in print as well as electronic form. Printing and mailing time added to the delay.

Overnight mailing was an option, but expensive. An idea blossomed. The RFP did not specify that the contractor had to supply the print copies, only that the scientists wanted print copies. Electronic transfer of the information. Instead of printing search results, they could be sent electronically to the remote sites. Those scientists who needed paper copies could print it on their own.

"Now, let me see, where is that description of the computer capabilities at the sites we're to serve?" Excitement now driving her actions, Hayley found the documents and read them through.

It was as she had remembered. All research facilities had at least one networked printer, and the DEP stated that each scientist would have a laptop connected to the internal network by the start of the contract. The results could be transmitted directly to the user. And with the information in an electronic format, the scientists could set up their own information files if they wanted.

Now, which document management system could do it? She remembered that Maggie had mentioned last week that she had seen a demonstration of a system used at one of the colleges in town. Hayley grabbed her notes and the proposal specifications and headed for Maggie's office. Within an hour, they had located equipment and software requirements for a system.

"This is a great idea," Maggie exclaimed, echoing Hayley's excitement. "It's bypassing a lot of paper and giving the scientists more capability than they had before. Good job!" Hayley beamed under her supervisor's praise. "We are going to need copyright agreements from each database vendor for the transfer of the information. I can look into that. And we have to make sure that all this hardware and software is compatible. That's your job. Get Jeff to look over the configuration. If he says it's all right, write it up."

Not only did Jeff think that the equipment and software were compatible, he went so far as to say that he could use the whole set-up for the other projects in the company that relied on the delivery of text across long distances. He and Hayley spent two hours ironing out the details, and Hayley spent Saturday morning in her office, writing up the general outline of the service and collecting more résumés. By one in the afternoon she had slipped her section onto the growing pile on Louise's desk.

The rest of the weekend lay before Hayley like a wide desert. She had a hundred little things to do — laundry, dusting, working on a new kite, reading, writing to her brothers — but none of those things grabbed her interest. She wanted to spend time with David, she admitted to herself. For now, the little things would have to do.

She worked on a new kite that evening and tested it on Sunday. But the late-morning experience was disappointing at best. The wind wasn't right. The kite's balance wasn't right. She wasn't right. Every action in the park reminded her of another kite launched in a spring breeze. She caught herself watching for a tall, lithe figure more than the kite, and finally she gave up.

Later, on her way to the kite room, as Hayley had dubbed her second bedroom, she flipped on the radio. As the music of *The Sound of Music* burst into the room, Hayley laughed in delight. The day was not a total waste. At least she had not missed her favorite weekly radio program that presented Broadway musical soundtracks. While she hung the recalcitrant kite among the dozen in the room, she hummed along with the radio. Satisfied that her worktable was clear, she went back out to the kitchen to consider lunch.

She had pulled lettuce, cucumbers, and tomatoes out of the refrigerator when the phone rang. Still humming, she turned the radio down and picked up the receiver. "Hello?"

"Hello, Hayley?"

The voice was vaguely familiar. After a second's hesitation, Hayley decided it was a male voice, but the sound was so scratchy, she swallowed before answering.

"Yes, this is she."

"This is David. I need you to come over—"

"David?" Hayley broke in, more concerned with his voice than surprised by his call. "You sound terrible! What on earth is wrong with your voice?"

"I caught a cold. The first thing that goes is my throat."

"I can hardly recognize you."

"Well, it's me." His irritation crackled over the line. "I don't think I can make it to work tomorrow, and I have some of the revisions for the Best and Final. I can't get Louise on the phone. Could you come over and pick these up?" By the end of his request, his voice had dropped to a whisper, and Hayley cringed.

"I'll do anything you want, as long as you get better. I can't stand to listen to you."

That produced a chuckle over the line. "When can I expect you?"

"You live at Park Plaza, don't you?" Hayley mentally began the estimation.

"Yes."

"About twenty minutes, then. I'm going to bike over. Is there a place to lock a bicycle up?"

"Check with the reception desk." With that thankfully short explanation and his unit number, David hung up. Hayley had soon unlocked her bicycle and was pedaling in the light Sunday traffic through Oakland.

As she wound her way through the residential streets to the established condominium complex, Hayley had time to deal with her rising anticipation at seeing David again. At last. A chance to judge his feelings toward her. She thanked the flu that had been flying around the office. This meeting just might give her some idea of how to approach David Mansfield in the future.

CHAPTER 11

Hayley had no trouble locating the imposing brick building with its curved driveway and rows of windows marking off ten stories of living space. After checking in with reception, she wheeled her bike into the elevator and pushed 7. The doors closed, and the elevator rose quietly to the seventh floor, settling with a light jerk. She maneuvered out into the bright hallway, found the correct door, and knocked. After a long pause, the door swung open.

One glance told her that here, indeed, was a sick man. David's skin looked gray in the hallway light, and his hair rioted over his head in a rare show of freedom. He wore a plaid robe over flannel pajamas. In one hand, he held a tissue box, while the other hand held a single, crumpled tissue. Just as Hayley was about to say hello, David's body was wracked with a sneeze, then another. He motioned her into the room then applied his energies to blowing his nose.

Hayley gently leaned the bike against the wall in the entryway and closed the door. When David finally raised his head from the tissue, Hayley could barely see the blue in his eyes for the redness and the watery film.

David threw the box on a table and walked toward a doorway on his right. "I was just putting everything together," he croaked.

As she followed David in, Hayley's first impression of the condo was the overwhelming sense of light. Stark white walls ended in gleaming hardwood floors. The only furnishings in the room were a huge, black leather sofa, three low, glass end tables, and a few throw rugs of white woven cotton. Narrow floor-to-ceiling windows to her right washed the room with afternoon sunlight. For all the brightness, Hayley felt uncomfortable.

She walked slowly to the dining area through which David had disappeared, noting the oak dining set with sleek modern lines. Here she realized the reason for her discomfort. There was no sign of life in these rooms. No magazines thrown on the couch, no knickknacks, no plants, no trophies.

In the dining room, the only sign of David's presence was a large photograph mounted on the wall. After a moment, Hayley recognized it as a time-exposure of molten slag being dumped down the hillside from one of the steel plants south of town. Slag was no longer disposed of in this cavalier manner, but when she was a little girl, her mother had told her stories of ending visits to Pittsburgh with a late-night excursion to the hills to watch for dumping. The picture matched her mother's description of the rivers of red and yellow streaked against the black hillside. Only the light from the slag exposed the outline of the mountain. The photograph was a statement of man's advancement in technology and a moment of unleashed power caught in the camera's eyes.

David's kiss flashed through her mind. The emotion he evoked was like that slag, fiery and uncontrolled. She wrapped her arms around her waist, suddenly shivering with yearning.

"I think this is it," David's scratchy voice swung her around. He dropped the pile of paper on the table and focused his attention on getting the loose paper into a manila envelope.

Hayley took the time to control her shivering. A group of papers fell from his fingers to scatter across the table. Hayley moved instinctively to help, and her hand brushed his.

David jerked away as if he had been burned.

Hayley froze. She faced him, not trying to disguise the hurt and bewilderment in her eyes.

David searched her face for a moment, then his jaw tensed in determination, and he began to gather the papers together again.

Hayley moved away from him, afraid to touch him, afraid to be rejected.

"I appreciate this," David said as the last of the paper slipped safely into the envelope. "I wouldn't ask unless it was absolutely necessary."

The knife in her stomach rotated one more twist. "I know," Hayley answered calmly. "I don't mind." Then she smiled to loosen her tension. "I look on it as a good deed."

David's eyebrows rose in question.

"No one else has to listen to you talk."

David smirked. At that moment, a high whistle shrieked from the kitchen.

"My tea", David said as Hayley looked around in alarm. He disappeared through swinging doors at the end of the room. Curious to see the rest of his living space, Hayley followed.

Again, the decor in the narrow kitchen was in the best of taste — white cabinets trimmed in blue, ceramic tiles in a blue Delft pattern on the backsplash, white tile on the floor, a chrome sink, and a wall-mounted breakfast bar with two polished wooden stools for seating. There the taste ended. Dishes cluttered the breakfast bar. Dried egg and something that resembled flour paste spotted the butcher-block countertops. Every available space was covered by a pan or glass, and a gaily colored potholder or towel completed the confusion. To pour the water for tea, David had cleared a spot by shoving a pile of dishes across the counter.

In an instant, all of Hayley's training from the *cleanliness freak* as she and her brothers called her mother, came bubbling to the top of her being.

"This is a disaster," she cried. "How on earth can you live like this?"

At her outburst, David jumped, and a generous amount of hot water splashed over the countertop as well as over his hand. He yelped, set the teapot back on the burner with deliberate care, and rounded on Hayley.

"Could you manage to control your screaming? I'm trying to get a cup of tea, not get scalded."

"We're even now," Hayley said smugly and waited until he caught the reference to their first meeting. She continued with relish. "Serves you right. Any man who can let a kitchen wallow in this filth…" She lifted a dishrag from the top of the pile and took a whiff. "Ugh!"

"The housekeeper doesn't come in until Tuesday." In his anger, David's voice squeaked. "I have difficulty cleaning when I feel as if I've been dragged from a horse!" This sentence ended in a fit of coughing and sneezing that effectively closed the argument.

When David was able to bring his head out of the tissue, Hayley considered him with blatant sympathy. "I'm sorry. Here I am, ranting about the kitchen, and look at you. Have you had a decent meal today?"

"I couldn't even get a cup of tea," he snapped back.

"It's not my fault you're not coordinated," she stated, then silenced his protest with a firm order. "Now get to bed. I'll take care of the tea and something to eat. That is, if I can find anything in this mess," she added in an undertone.

"Hayley, I'd rather you didn't—"

Although it hurt to know he wanted to be rid of her, Hayley couldn't leave until she knew he was comfortable. A little assertiveness might be just the ticket. "Don't tell me what to do, David Mansfield. You may be the boss in the office, but you're in no condition to dictate to me here. Now get out and get some sleep."

As she had guessed, he was too weary to argue, and he shuffled from the kitchen. Now that he was out of the way, Hayley dug into her task. *What a mess!* she thought.

An apron, probably the housekeeper's, hung on a hook by the refrigerator. Hayley donned that and began to stack the dishes neatly in the dishwasher, setting those aside that were beyond mechanical help and would require a bit of elbow grease. When she had created some space on the counter, she searched until she found canned soup in the cupboard and discovered cold turkey in the refrigerator. More hunting revealed a pan for soup, bread and mayonnaise for the sandwiches, and oversized mugs and plates. Soon the soup was simmering, and she had made two sandwiches. She found a wooden tray and arranged everything on it, including silverware and paper napkins, which she'd uncovered when she had lifted a pile of dishes off the counter. Then she set out to find her patient.

She passed the swinging doors that led to the dining room and proceeded down the hall. On the left, she passed a bathroom and what she assumed was a second bedroom behind a closed door. The door on the right was open, and she entered. She could barely make out David's head under the green blanket on the queen-size bed, but she could hear him breathing steadily. She smiled at the picture he made then glanced around to see where she could set the tray. A compact rolling desk under the window was relatively clear so she moved to it. On top, she recognized papers from the proposal, some of Louise's notes, some of her own. There were reports from Jeff and

Eileen, and she spied a copy of the scientific background from Dr. Matt. The wire-rimmed glasses lay to the side.

This room was obviously where David lived. Photographs dotted the walls, presenting more evidence of his craft and the sensitivity in his use of shadows across an old woman's face or the shine in a small boy's eyes. Although the desk was a confusion of paper, David's clothes were hung neatly in the closet. The only exception was the suit slung over a side chair. Hayley recognized the jacket he had worn on Friday. He probably had not been feeling well even then. She took the opportunity to savor the impressions this room gave her. A combination of hard work with a knowing eye for people. The room felt so right.

With a sigh, Hayley called softly to the sleeping form. David woke instantly, jerking his head from the pillow to pin her with a blank stare. Then his eyes cleared as he remembered why she was there.

Hayley picked up the tray. "If you'll sit up, I'll put this on your lap."

He obeyed, and, after seeing him sip the steaming soup, Hayley turned and went back to the kitchen. Between his illness and his messages for her to stay away, the kitchen seemed to be the safest place. In a busy fifteen minutes, she set the rest of the dishes in the dishwasher and turned it on. She scrubbed the pans she had set aside and wiped down all the countertops. After surveying the greatly expanded surface area and certain she had stopped the growth of harmful bacteria, she went back to the bedroom to collect the tray.

He had just finished the tea and laid the cup down with a smile. "Thanks. I feel a hundred percent better already."

Hayley glowed at the thank you. "Your voice doesn't sound much better, but at least you have a little more color. Can I get you anything else?"

"No, that was quite enough. Anyway, I heard you out in the kitchen. I suppose you couldn't stand the mess."

"How could you tell?" They smiled over the memory of her reaction to the disorder. "I was raised by an obsessive-compulsive cleaner," Hayley explained. "Our neighbors used to wonder if we really had three children in the house or whether it was all a myth."

She leaned over to him and picked up the tray. "I'll take this back." She got to the door then paused, remembering the work on his desk. "May I ask you something?"

"Yes?"

"I saw the work on your desk for the Best and Final. I don't see how you're going to get all that done by Tuesday. You need to rest."

He crossed his arms in a clear sign of resolve. "I'll finish it."

"But I could compose the drafts for the revised sections—" Hayley insisted.

"No!" burst from him. "I don't want you near — uh — it!"

His slight fumble with the last word hurt Hayley, and a great sense of injustice swept over her. She set the tray down on the side chair and walked to stand at the end of the bed, arms crossed, her eyes fixed to his.

"I know you don't want me near you," she said, and drew a breath when his face revealed that she had hit the mark, "but I never thought there was any question of my capabilities at work."

The silence between them stretched. David's eyes softened. "No, there isn't."

"Then stop being stubborn and let me do this. I'll integrate all the notes into draft revisions, have Louise type it up, and leave it on your desk by Wednesday morning. That way, if you want to stay home on Tuesday you can. Wednesday should give you plenty of time to look over the revisions and make the final changes."

She thought for a moment he might refuse her offer, but finally he simply said, "All right."

Relieved by his answer, she picked up the tray. "I'll be back in a minute."

When she returned, David said, "The notes are right on top. But leave your ideas on the document conversion. I want to take more time with that."

Hayley's hands shook a little as she found the right papers. His request to spend more time with her ideas was a small concession for his earlier behavior, and she was thankful for his positive thoughts about her work.

"Hayley?"

The voice from the bed brought her around to face him. She waited for a moment, studying his face and the blue of his eyes. He seemed to want to tell her something, and Hayley's heart skipped a beat. He might be reconsidering their relationship.

In the end, he only said, "Thank you. For everything."

To cover her disappointment, Hayley shrugged. "No problem." She gathered the papers into her arms and headed for the door. "This will be on your desk by Wednesday."

He nodded, and she hurried back down the hall. As she untied the apron and took one last look around the kitchen, Hayley assessed the situation. She wanted to take care of him, and he couldn't bear to have her around. At least he admitted that her work was good. That had not changed. She wondered how long she could endure his decision to stay apart. As she dropped the envelope in the bicycle basket and prepared to make her way out the front door, she looked back upon the afternoon light playing on the hardwood floors.

As long as it takes, she vowed silently.

CHAPTER 12

Hayley immersed herself in the Best and Final revisions. The responsibility that she had assumed seemed tiny compared to her desire to please David and convince him that she could be trusted with his heart as well as his business. She posed questions to every team member, rewrote sections, requested more information, and proofread material flying from under Louise's nimble fingers. Two temporary typists had been hired to help during this final week of writing, and Hayley helped Louise coordinate the typing of the final draft. On Tuesday evening near eight o'clock, Hayley finally dropped the completed package on David's desk with a tired sigh. She would have felt elated if a haze of exhaustion had not been pulling at her every movement.

She arrived at work late on Wednesday and was unaware that David was in until she received a call from him early in the afternoon.

"We need to get together to go over some of the source material. How about tomorrow morning?"

"I can't," Hayley answered, clenching her fist around the phone. "I'll be gone for a few hours in the morning. I'm going to the dentist tomorrow. It takes months to get an appointment—"

"All right," David cut in, "tomorrow afternoon."

The icy tone broadcasted his irritation. Hayley tried to salvage what she could of the dilemma. "Tomorrow afternoon will be fine, but I'll bring up the material and notes I used. I should be back around eleven, and we can talk."

"Fine," was the clipped answer followed by a dead line.

Hayley went cold inside. *I've really done it this time*, she thought. Then she rallied. *I can't be responsible for the dentist's untenable schedule. The Best and Final will get done.* If she was any judge of the writing she had completed, David did not have much more work, so there was nothing to worry about. Still, her stomach stayed in a tight coil.

She gathered the notes she had used for the draft and took them up to Louise. Then she lost herself in searching for software prices. She was nearly ready to give up for the day, when the phone rang. Still, reading, she said, "Library."

"Hayley! Just who I needed." The boom of Peter's voice thrust her out of the prices and back into social reality.

"Peter. What a surprise!" she said with real pleasure. "I haven't heard from you in an age."

"That's the kind of reception a guy likes." Peter laughed. "I should leave you alone more often."

Hayley swallowed her shame. She had hardly thought of Peter for weeks, and the only reason she was glad to hear from him now was because he took her mind away from another male presence. She tried to ease her conscience by being enthusiastic. "No, you shouldn't. A girl doesn't like to be taken for granted."

"Never," Peter answered in mock dismay. "I'll make up for it right away. Dinner? Tonight?"

That's just what I need, Hayley thought. *A little attention from Peter.* "Sounds wonderful," she answered aloud.

"Great. Pick you up sevenish?"

"All right. See you then."

As the line went dead, Hayley grinned at the prospect of a break from this proposal and from her lonely apartment. *Funny,* she thought, *before that Sunday, I never thought of the apartment as lonely.*

When she got home, Hayley replaced the bead necklace she wore for a sterling silver chain and added silver earrings. The navy suit with the eggshell silk blouse would be suitable for anything Peter had planned.

The plan was simple. Peter chose a steakhouse in the Oakland area decorated with a Casablanca flavor — wicker tables and chairs, bamboo screens, slowly whirling ceiling fans, and a piano player weaving soft music. They ate their steaks while chatting amicably, and Hayley felt a warm lethargy soothe her body.

"You seem a bit down tonight," Peter said. "Was your steak all right?"

The question roused her out of her haze. "Oh, the steak was delicious. I'm just tired. And this is so relaxing."

"More relaxing then the Best and Final, I'll bet."

Haley became fully alert at that comment. "How do you know that?"

"Mansfield knows I'm in, doesn't he?"

"Yes..." Hayley drew the word out, suddenly unsure of Peter's motives.

Peter laughed. "You're absolutely right. Contractors are not supposed to know who else is bidding. But you know how small contracting circles are. How can one plan if one doesn't know the competition?"

Hayley smiled with Peter at the facetious statement. "True. I'm just not accustomed to all this talk of secrecy when everyone knows exactly what's happening anyway."

Peter leaned on his elbows and took her hands. "Ah, but here is the fun part. I know that David Mansfield is in the Best and Final. I may even be able to guess at the kind of procedures he will propose. But I don't know the details. Who is he hiring? Has he got better computer software to handle this project? How much capital does he really have? Trying to find out is the best game in town."

Hayley bristled. "And someone on the inside might be willing to play." She withdrew her hands. "Think again, buddy."

"Hayley!" Peter exclaimed and retrieved one hand. "Perish the thought! We've been through this before, and I promised I wouldn't pry. Let's dance before you accuse me of more sinister motives in bringing you here tonight."

Hayley flushed in embarrassment. It wasn't like her to jump to conclusions. She was tired — that was it. She took Peter's outstretched hand and gave him a grateful smile for understanding her position. To the soft strains of an old love song crooning from the piano, she and Peter began to sway in slow rhythm. Hayley had always found Peter to be an excellent dancer, smooth and light on his feet. Tonight he held her close and moved with easy grace, but Hayley felt smothered. She fought the breathlessness down. There was no reason to be uneasy with Peter.

"Oh, Hayley," Peter whispered near her ear," I could go on like this forever. Having you in my arms like this. Maybe not forever," he amended with a sigh, "but certainly for my lifetime."

Panic bubbled inside Hayley. She pushed herself off his chest to achieve a safe distance. "Peter, please, not tonight."

Peter searched her face in disappointment and surprise. "What is it? You know how I feel."

"Peter, I just…"

Before Hayley could complete the protest and formulate an answer he deserved, the voice that plagued her both day and night rose beside them.

"Well, Jameson. Out on the town tonight, I see. With all the work that must go into your bid, I don't know how you can afford the time."

The president of Mansfield Inc. was beside them and, to Hayley's chagrin, not alone. Hayley could honestly say that David's companion did not impress her from the neck up. But from the neck down — Hayley knew an invitation when she saw one. The flowing jersey dress rippled over the woman's ample figure, and the plunging neckline stopped just short of indecent.

Hayley had stiffened at the sound of the voice, but after a quick appraisal of the situation, she focused her eyes on the buttonhole in Peter's jacket lapel.

In answer to David's comment, Peter glanced pointedly at Hayley and said, "I'd say the sacrifice was worth it."

"We'll see when the bids are in," David stated in a voice as cold as ice.

Peter gave a curt laugh and swung Hayley out of range toward another corner of the dance floor. "We certainly will see," he mumbled.

In Peter's embrace, Hayley fought the wave of hurt and jealousy caused by the sight of someone else in David's arms. She tightened her grip on Peter hoping to transfer some of the pain to his broad frame. Peter responded by drawing her closer.

"No matter what, I'll say it's worth it," he said and gently kissed Hayley's hair.

In her pain, Hayley realized that it had been a mistake to see Peter. Her feelings could not — and never would — match his.

With the strength of newfound knowledge behind her, Hayley said, "Can we get out of here, Peter?"

Peter pulled away to peer into her face. "Are you all right?"

I'm far from all right, Hayley thought, but to him, shook her head. "I'll be better when I can get some air." She raised her eyes to him so he could see the plea in them. "Please."

Peter's arm was around her shoulders. "Sure, sure."

Somehow she survived the process of paying the bill, and pulled her coat around her shoulders. The vision of David's arms around an overdeveloped body hung before her, and she felt physically ill. Finally, they were out in the clear, cool air, and Hayley's vision began to be replaced with reality.

So wrapped up in her own thoughts, Hayley did not notice that Peter had not started the car. She was just grateful to be able to breathe again. Finally she sensed Peter's gaze on her and turned to look at him.

"What's wrong?" he asked, his concern tingeing the question.

Hayley clasped her hands together, shrugged in what she hoped would be a nonchalant manner, and looked out the front window at the moon rising over the dark mountains. "I was surprised to see David there. He usually doesn't go out when a big proposal is due."

"And that accounts for this reaction? Sorry, Hayley, it doesn't wash. You look like you've lost your last friend."

Hayley forced herself to sit still while Peter's eyes studied her. At last, he asked the question that Hayley feared and expected.

"Is there something going on between you and Mansfield?"

The pain of the last weeks surged through her answer. "Not anymore."

Peter was silent for so long that Hayley finally turned her head. His hands clutched the steering wheel then relaxed.

A laughing couple got into the car next to Peter's in the parking lot and shot off in a roar of power. In the silence that descended, Peter shifted in his seat to face Hayley. His hand cupped her chin, and he held her face in the dim light, his eyes locked to hers.

"Why did you come with me tonight?"

Hayley squeezed her hands together until they hurt. "For all the wrong reasons," she answered, trying, no matter the consequences, for the truth. "To get away from my apartment for a while. To forget about work. To forget about him."

Peter dropped his hand and whispered, "So that's the way the wind lies."

"I love him, Peter."

"But he doesn't love you."

Hayley hesitated then decided on a small lie. "Obviously not."

Peter caught the hesitation. "Or he does, and he doesn't know it. What a fool!" he exclaimed through clenched teeth.

"He's been hurt before," Hayley stated, surprised that she could still defend him, but intuitively knowing that Peter would understand.

He nodded, and his answer confirmed Hayley's guess. "It's a shame he hasn't dealt with that yet." A silence fell again, this time less tense. "Where does that leave us?" he finally asked.

It was Hayley's turn to sigh. Why was life so painful?

"I wish I knew," she said. Then she laid her hand on Peter's sleeve. "I care for you a great deal. As a friend, I could ask for none better." A bitter laugh from her companion drove Hayley to move closer to him and, with her hand against his cheek, turn his face to her so she could see his eyes. "Right now, I don't know what to do. I'm not so naïve that I'll carry a torch forever. I think there's still a chance for David and me. I need some time."

Peter turned away from her touch. "Why is it always this way? David and I tearing at each other? Why do I feel I'll be competing with him for the rest of my life?"

Peter's hurt words cut into Hayley's heart. Anger welled up in her, anger at David for not pursuing the truth five years ago and for perpetuating the gulf between him and Peter.

"I told him, and I'll tell you," Hayley said firmly. "This is not a competition. I am not the prize in some chariot race or duel."

Her words had the desired effect. Peter laughed quietly and put his arm around her. "You're right. I have to stop seeing my whole life as a battle with J. D. He may see his life that way, but I don't need to follow his example." He gently kissed Hayley on the brow. Then Peter caught up Hayley's hands in his. "I'll wait for you to straighten things out. I'm here — the friend you've described, more than a friend if you'll have me. I'll wait until you can decide."

For the first time in several of their meetings, Hayley felt completely comfortable with Peter. She drew her arms around him and gave him a tight hug. "Thanks so much for understanding."

A kiss was Peter's reply. Then he started the motor and drove Hayley home.

CHAPTER 13

Hayley spent Thursday morning in the dentist's office. The annual exam was bad enough, but the interminable waiting tested Hayley's patience to the limit. When she finally left, she decided to have lunch before going back to work. She wouldn't dare try to deal with David on an empty stomach. After a tuna salad sandwich and crisp apple, Hayley felt prepared to put in a long afternoon.

As Hayley expected, Maggie greeted her with "He wants to see you right away."

"No rest for the wicked," Hayley sighed. She flipped through the mail on her desk, then she grabbed a notebook and headed for the tenth floor.

Louise stopped her before Hayley could get into the inner office.

"I don't know what's happened," Louise said in a hushed voice, "but he's unbearable. I'd better let him know you're here. I don't want you to walk in on anything."

Hayley only nodded. If Louise was being cautious, then things behind the door were grim.

"Hayley's here," Louise said after knocking on the door and opening it. Hayley heard no reply from within, but Louise must have gotten a signal, because she stepped back to let Hayley pass.

"Good luck," Louise whispered.

As the door slid shut behind her, Hayley took a deep breath. David stood at the wall of windows behind his desk, a lone, dark figure against the glare of the afternoon sun. Even with the length of the room between them, Hayley could see his tension in the set of his neck and shoulders. Waves of energy surrounded her as his silence stretched for several seconds. When he finally turned, Hayley's heart stopped then pounded slowly. David's eyes radiated cold fury.

He threw the manila envelope in his hands across the desk at her. "Explain this."

Hayley approached the envelope warily. She lifted it, noted that there was no address label or markings on the outside, and drew out the contents. In a folder was a short note written on Mansfield stationary imprinted with her name. The note read, *Peter, this should be all you need to win.* Attached was a copy of the proposal section on document conversion.

Hayley shook her head slowly and looked up.

David's eyes raked over her. "Did you write that note?" he asked with deadly calm.

Hayley looked at it again and began the denial when memory rushed through her. She had written the note just weeks ago. She started to explain but stopped at the look on David's face. He had paled. His eyes were almost black with pain.

"You did write it," he whispered.

Hayley rushed her words. "Yes, I wrote it. Weeks ago."

"So you were sending him information even then?"

"No! Please. Listen. Peter had a trivia bet with a friend of his. What was the smallest city in Pennsylvania. He asked me if I'd help. I found the answer in an almanac of state facts."

"That doesn't explain how this note came to be on your desk this morning," David cut in.

"I don't know. I do remember that after I had written the note, it got misplaced on my desk. You know how my desk is. So I wrote another one, thinking I had thrown away the first." He was shaking his head in disbelief and even to Hayley the excuse sounded contrived. "I know it sounds impossible, but that's what happened. I never gave the first note another thought."

"You really expect me to believe your story? Come on. If you're clever enough to get the stuff out of here, you should be able to devise a better story."

Frustration seethed through every blood vessel in Hayley's body. David truly thought that she was passing information, and clearly it would take more than her word to convince him. "If I was that clever, I wouldn't leave something like that lying around," she said. "Think about it. I'd have to be pretty stupid to leave it… where did you find it? On my desk? In plain view?"

The anger and pain that had flown over his face were replaced by coldness. "Not stupid. Perhaps careless."

The coldness hurt Hayley more than anything else. "David, don't do this," she pleaded.

"Don't do what?" David lashed back.

Hayley flinched as if he had struck her.

"Don't acknowledge what is clear to the world? That I have a thief working for me?"

Hayley edged around the desk toward him, acting on the hope that her nearness might bring him to his senses if the facts as he knew them would not. "But why?" she argued. "Why would I steal from you?"

David smiled with a show of teeth like a wounded animal. "Maybe you felt rejected. Unrequited love?"

The words struck Hayley like a bullet. Her face drained of color, and she grasped the edge of the desk to keep from collapsing, her eyes locked to his. "How can you believe that?" she whispered.

David's pain reverberated through his words. "Do you think I want to? Do you think I want to believe any of this? Do you think I want to brand you as a thief? You, of all people? Give me something. Tell me you haven't been seeing Jameson regularly. Tell me you didn't write the note." His hands clutched her shoulders. "Give me some proof."

Hayley squared her shoulders and stepped out of his reach. "You have my word."

"It's not enough."

Hayley stared at him while her emotions congealed into stone. There was no softness in his eyes, no sign that he doubted the evidence even a little. He did not trust her now. He never would.

Without conscious thought, but with a good deal of conviction, she said, "You will have my resignation before five today."

Her hand was on the doorknob when his voice stopped her. "I didn't ask for it."

She turned and leaned against the door for support in making a decision to face the truth about the two of them, even if it tore them apart forever. "Now that I know what type of person you are, I consider my leaving inevitable."

"And what type of person is that?"

"A coward," she stated. His eyes shot open, and she nodded. "It's easier for you to believe that flimsy evidence than it is to take a chance that I might be right, to find out the truth no matter what. Just like it was easier to push Peter out of your life than to face the truth about your wife. It was easier to walk out on me that weekend than to try something new and wonderful." David's face was white, but Hayley could not stop the words that tumbled out. "Go ahead. Keep pushing everyone away who cares for you. Keep the world at arm's length. One day you'll try to push, and all you'll feel is air. I can't live like that. I didn't think you could either. Good-bye, David."

She left, knowing that her shaking would soon overtake her words and actions. The suffering and anger on his face would be with her always. She closed the door solidly behind her and leaned back against it, her rage and disappointment forcing her breath out in short gasps.

Louise sprang from the chair to take Hayley's arm. "What's wrong? What happened?"

Hayley thrust herself from the door. "You'd better ask him." She fumbled in her jacket pocket, finally bringing out her key ring. With jerky movements, she wrenched her office and desk keys off the ring. "I won't be needing these anymore."

She dropped the keys into Louise's open palm and looked up to meet the older woman's stunned expression. "I'll call you later." Hayley pressed Louise's fingers around the keys and squeezed. "I'm in no condition to talk about it now."

Hayley strode to the library out of habit. She did not pause to think of the consequences of what she had just done, or of the future. She forced herself to act, to finish four months of her life, to do the little things that would take her away from the man in the tenth-floor office as quickly as possible.

She sat at the computer and typed a one-sentence resignation addressed to Maggie with a copy to J. David Mansfield. She would have to talk to Maggie. She couldn't just leave. She printed an envelope for David and slid his copy into it. She cleared a corner of her desk to lay the second copy down. She considered it for a minute, her mind echoing the words. *I resign my position... resign my position...*

She roused herself and searched for a box in the library. Into the box, she threw the telephone notepad she had brought from library school, a picture of her brothers, personal files. Anything remotely related to Mansfield Inc. she tossed on the desk. Only four months, yet there was a lot accumulated. She sat at the computer and started reviewing her electronic contacts file. She'd need names and phone numbers if she were going to find another job. The thought stabbed her a moment, then a rush of anger propelled her to export the entire file onto a flash drive.

The phone rang. Hayley yanked the receiver to her ear. "Yes?"

A pause hung in the air then came a tentative, "May I speak to Hayley, please?"

She let out her breath. "It's me, Peter."

"It is? Was it something I said?"

A chuckle, wrung with bitterness, escaped her. "No. This was thanks to your friend, J. D. Mansfield."

"Ah, not pleased with the Best and Final."

Hayley sank into her chair and pressed her forehead against her hands. "Not pleased with me." She lifted her head to see Maggie standing just inside the door. "I just quit."

Maggie's eyes widened, and she took a step toward Hayley.

Hayley stopped her with an upraised palm.

After a pause, Peter said, "You're joking."

Hayley squeezed the phone but said nothing.

"What are you going to do?"

"I don't know. It was just five minutes ago. I haven't gotten that far yet," Hayley answered in irritation, her eyes fixed on Maggie's colorless face.

"Why, for pity's sake, did you quit?" Peter exclaimed in her ear.

With Maggie standing in front of her, Hayley hesitated. Everyone would know soon enough. Why be secretive about it now? "He accused me of breaking company confidentiality. Guess who was my accomplice?"

Now the silence drew out into seconds. "Me," Peter said, resignation enveloping the word like a shroud. "I'm sorry, Hayley. If it had been any other guy—"

"Don't kid yourself, Peter," Hayley said. "David Mansfield is not the trusting type. It wouldn't have mattered who it was."

Peter did not respond.

"Hey," Hayley said lightly, cutting the silence that threatened to choke her. "Did you bring your car downtown today?"

"Yes."

"Can I get a ride home? I've got this box of stuff that I'd rather not manage on the bus."

Peter attempted to match her tone. "Sure. What time will you be ready?"

"About an hour?"

"Three-thirty, then. In front of your building."

"Fine. I'll be there."

"Good. And Hayley?"

"Yes?"

"Chin up. We'll work this out somehow."

"Right," she said and hung up. There was nothing left to work out, except the rest of her life.

Meeting Maggie's eyes again, Hayley motioned apologetically to the phone. "Sorry. I had wanted to talk with you first." She handed her supervisor the letter.

Maggie read it, folded the paper, and shrugged. "Talk to me now. Did he really accuse you?"

Hayley nodded. "I tried to explain, but—"

Maggie sighed. "I've been here for over three years, and he's always been scrupulously fair. But this company is his weakness. He's never rational if it's threatened. It's just as well that you go now, before you end up in a battle that no one wins."

Hayley looked at her quizzically. "You think he was wrong." The statement ended in a question even though there was no inflection in Hayley's voice.

"I know you didn't give Peter anything," Maggie said with a small smile. "I think I know a little bit about people, and you're as straight as they come. You'll have no trouble getting another job, and without David, you'll probably be better off."

Hayley only nodded. The phrase *without David* had hit her stomach. This meant that she would not see him again. Not spend hours writing. Not look up from her desk to see him standing in the window watching her. *Don't think!* she admonished herself roughly. *Act!*

She whirled to the wall and unpinned the cat poster from the bulletin board. There would be no more Fridays in this office. She rolled up the poster, snapped a rubber band around it, and threw it into the box. She looked around again and pulled a young spider plant from the top of the filing cabinet and added it to the box. She set her hands on either side of the carton and studied it. "Well, that's all, I guess."

"Not quite," Maggie said.

Hayley looked at her.

"If you need a reference for your next job, don't hesitate to use my name."

A cloud over Hayley lifted at Maggie's offer. She smiled in relief and gratefulness. "Thanks."

Maggie held out her hand, and Hayley took it then moved around the desk to give her supervisor a quick hug. "Thanks for everything. I've learned so much here."

"You're very welcome." Maggie dropped her arms and assumed a business demeanor. "Well, you'd better fill me in on the DEP proposal so at least I can find something in this office."

A chuckle escaped Hayley. In the next half hour, she explained how she had arranged her files.

Maggie glanced at her watch. "You'd better go. Peter will be waiting, and all he'll get for his trouble is a ticket."

Hayley laughed. "That's all I need. To argue with another man today. Who knows what would happen?"

It was easier to leave then, with a laugh instead of awkwardness.

At the elevator, Maggie repeated her offer. "Use my name. I'm sure you'll get something soon."

With her arms around the box, Hayley could only nod as she stepped into the elevator. "I will. Thanks."

Peter leaped out of the coupe as soon as he saw her and lifted the burden out of her arms. "I was just about to take another turn around the block," he shouted over the blare of horns and rumble of cars. The trunk stood open, and he placed the box in it as Hayley slipped into the passenger side. When Peter joined her, he took in her face with a swift appraising glance. "You okay?"

"For the moment," Hayley answered, surprised that it was no less than the truth. She should feel something other than this light-headed mist, but for now she was fine.

"Well, I have an idea. If you agree, we're going to Malloy's to get a beer. I could use one, even if you can't."

Hayley grinned. "I can use one. Malloy's sounds great."

The establishment was an under lit student pub known for its cheap beer and deep booths, where many an intimate conversation was held amid general clamor and rowdiness.

When they settled in a booth with frosty mugs chilling their hands, Peter said, "So tell me the rest."

Between sips of beer, Hayley recounted her afternoon — David's anger, her despair, and disappointment in his attitude. When she finished, the silence stretched for several minutes.

"I'd offer to talk to him—" Peter began.

"But he wouldn't listen to you." Hayley smiled. "Sad, but true."

As Peter leaned back against the leather booth, he laid his hand over hers on the table. "What are you going to do?"

"Find another job, I guess." It was a simple statement, implying a simple process. Hayley knew it was not, but was not ready to face that reality today. Peter's eyes watched her placidly, and she added as much for herself as for him, "I won't go back."

"I should hope not." Peter squeezed her hand. After a moment, his eyes lit, and he said, "I have an idea. Come work for me."

Hayley laughed. "Oh, Peter, be serious."

"I *am* serious. I know you're good. Mansfield never would have gotten to the Best and Final without you. And Ellen's been asking for help…" he finished almost to himself.

Alarmed at the direction this was going, Hayley stopped him. "Peter, no. How would it look?"

His eyes shot to hers. He repeated in astonishment, "'How would it look?' To whom?" Hayley flushed but held his gaze. "You mean you still care what he thinks? After today?"

"No," Hayley exclaimed, but even to her, the denial was too quick. "Yes, I care," she stated more quietly.

With a snort of disgust, Peter withdrew his hand and stared at her as if she had grown horns.

"He's not being cruel because he's a cruel person, Peter. He's protecting what he values most right now." Hayley raised her hand to stop Peter's protest. "Yes, I know he was unreasonable, but I can understand his position. I'm not any less hurt, and I certainly can't work for him again, but I *can* understand… and love him."

"I don't believe what I'm hearing." Peter's voice rose.

Quietly, Hayley repeated, "I love him. Just like you do."

Denial swept through Peter's face, and Hayley said, "The truth."

Peter nodded and laughed softly. "One thing you can say for J. D. Mansfield — he knows how to put the hooks in."

Hayley shared a smile with him. "And we're fools for letting him."

"Now that that's settled, I'll begin again. Why don't you work for me?"

"Peter!"

He lifted a finger to silence her. "With a slight modification. Let's say it's temporary. Ellen, my Information Specialist, has a few small projects begging to be done, and she can't get to them. There are some journal subscriptions to set up, a searchable news clippings file she mentioned, some indexing — a few months' work. You could look for another job, leave when you want to."

The glass revolved in Hayley's hands. "I do need the money," she murmured, arguing with herself.

"Aha!" Peter said with glee. "Another good reason."

Hayley laughed then studied the beer as she considered her options. She had been told it was easier to find a job while you were working. *But if I work for Peter, David will think he was right. Do I care what that man thinks? Yes, but I need to eat.* She looked at Peter and smiled. "All right." At the excitement that flooded Peter's face, she hurriedly added, "On one condition."

Light dancing in his eyes, Peter nodded. "Name it."

"I will have nothing to do with the DEP proposal. I will not help you with yours, and I will not tell you what's in Mansfield's submission."

Peter regarded her with narrowed eyes then sat back and whistled. "Lady, you drive a hard bargain."

Hayley ignored his reaction. She held out her hand across the table. "Agreed?"

After a moment's hesitation, Peter took the hand. "Agreed."

The tension slid from her shoulders, and Hayley relaxed against the booth and sipped the beer.

"Do you have a current résumé?" Peter asked, at once the businessman.

"We've gone through all this, and you want a résumé?"

Peter grinned sheepishly. "Well, I have to stick to the formalities for Ellen's sake. She doesn't like to be railroaded into anything."

"I don't blame her."

Hours later, as Hayley looked out the window of her apartment onto the tiny flower garden that moved like colored cloth in the evening breezes, she marveled that in this day, she had lost a job and gained a job, lost a boss and gained a boss. In her mind, she saw David's face, flushed with anger, and felt his voice slicing through her heart: "*It's not enough.*"

"Oh, David," she whispered to the flowers. "Why couldn't you trust me?"

CHAPTER 14

Three weeks after resigning from Mansfield, Hayley admitted that accepting Peter's offer had been the right decision. She liked the bustling Ellen, who gave extremely clear instructions, but often misplaced her glasses or coffee mug. The tasks were as Peter had said — short-term but mentally demanding. The nature of the work and her agreement with Peter permitted her to answer job ads and take off for interviews. Ellen was so glad to have help that she agreed to almost any arrangement Hayley suggested. Hayley settled into the transition time with optimism.

This morning Hayley had just arrived at her desk when Peter walked into the library. The sun streaming through the window dimmed a little when Hayley noticed the solemn expression on Peter's face. Apprehension kept her still until he reached her.

"I came to let you know that Mansfield won the DEP contract."

A jumble of feelings tangled in her. Pleasure flooded Hayley as if she had never left Mansfield and had every right to be proud of the work she had done. Her eyes brightened, and she flushed with joy.

"Oh, Peter," she said, a little breathless with the enormity of her accomplishment. Then she remembered where she was, for whom she worked now, and that she would not be able to develop the proposal into reality. She also recognized that Peter must be disappointed, and she clamped down on the excitement to add another, more quiet, "I'm sorry."

Peter sat in the chair next to her and took her hand. "I'm sorry, too, Hayley," he said earnestly. "You should have been there."

Her heart swelled. Peter was sensitive enough to know her disappointment. "But you lost the contract," she protested.

"But you lost a good deal more."

She turned from him to stare out the window into the afternoon sunlight. She was in David's office again, looking over plans, talking about services and the people. Peter's voice nudged her out of the daydream.

"I have meetings all day, and I leave for Washington early tomorrow, so I wanted to wish you luck on your interview on Thursday."

Hayley mustered a smile from among the range of emotions playing in her. "Thanks. I'll need it."

"Less than you think," he said affectionately and squeezed her hand. "I'll want to hear all about it." He glanced at his watch. "Gotta run. I'll call you or stop over as soon as I get back."

"All right. Have a good trip."

Peter kissed her on the cheek and, with a wave, left her to return to the indexing. But the work faded into the background of her mind as she imagined the excitement and bustle that must be gripping everyone at the Mansfield organization by now. She clasped her hands together in sudden frustration and shoved the chair away from the desk to pace to the window and back.

She had accepted not seeing David every day. She had even accepted the loss of the relationship. What she still regretted was the loss of the opportunity to work on the project that had been her plan and dream. Anger shook her as it so often did these days, and she silently cursed the man who could be so strong and confident in business, but so miserable in his closest personal relationships. Finally, the wave of anger subsided into resignation. She wasn't going to dwell on the waste of it all. She left Mansfield to escape a situation that was impossible. The decision had been made.

Hayley left work early on Thursday to have a long lunch and a break before her interview. While freshening up in the bathroom, she realized that she had forgotten her lipstick at home. A glance at her watch told her that she had enough time for a quick run into Kaufmann's, and there she might also pick up some of the specialty cologne she had meant to purchase a week ago.

The department store was crowded with lunch-time shoppers. Hayley wove her way among the people and counters to Cosmetics and made her purchases with little fuss. She stopped long enough to reassure herself that the receipts were in the bag when a deep voice caught her attention.

Directly across from her stood David Mansfield. He was leaning over the opposite case and pointing to the glass as the clerk pulled out the desired item.

His appearance so close to her stunned Hayley. He was smiling at the salesclerk, and Hayley bit her lip. He had smiled at her like that once. As she watched, he glanced up in her direction, and his smile froze. Then it faded, and the gleam in his eyes dimmed. He gave her a thoughtful nod, his eyes searching her face. Finally, he turned his attention back to his purchase.

Hayley had believed that she had mastered her emotions, but that one bland gesture tore through her heart. His opinion of her had not changed. Nothing had changed. She gathered up her package and purse and walked quickly from the store and into the noon crowds on the street.

Although she thrust David out of her mind long enough to survive the interview without saying something completely out of place, when she stepped out into the afternoon drizzle, he appeared in her thoughts again.

She grew to acknowledge his presence there in the weeks that followed. The smell of rain brought back to her the afternoon in the car when he had told her about Julia. The sound of an accordion player in Point Park reminded her of the Tamburitzans. An ice cube that escaped her glass and slithered down her leg recalled the Sunday afternoon when she had burned her hand. David was everywhere, sneaking in when she least expected it. She had hoped that he might come to her after learning that he had won the contract. But, except for the chance meeting in Kaufmann's, she had not seen him.

With no job on the horizon and an unfamiliar lethargy hanging over her, Hayley felt immense relief when her parents phoned to remind her that she had promised to visit soon. Determined to leave the city before her lassitude turned into serious depression, Hayley chose a week in late July and arranged to borrow a friend's car. She told her parents that she would indeed visit, but that she would spend time at the summer cottage first.

Peter sent her off with a kiss and an admonishment to have a good time. As she drove north out of the city and into the less-populated mountains, Hayley felt the oppression leave her, and she promised herself that she would have fun.

Upon her arrival at the small frame cottage, Hayley took time only to drop her suitcases in the front room and walked swiftly through the kitchen at the back of the house and out the screened porch to the sloping glade that spread to a finger of Conneaut Lake, fifty yards away. A gentle breeze stirred the humid air around her, and she settled near the lakeshore, feeling at peace with the world for the first time in many weeks.

For the next three days, she did nothing. At least nothing that could be described as constructive. She ate when she felt hungry, read, slept, spent hours on the bank staring at the water and the sky, and hiked miles of shoreline. She would have believed that the change of scenery had cured her of one J. David Mansfield had it not been for the dreams. Perfectly vivid, they engaged her emotions and senses into tableaus made up of reality, yet not real. David arguing with her over wording of the proposal then taking her into his arms and kissing her, holding her tight.

One evening after dinner, she chose to sit on the lakeshore, her thoughts weaving sleepily around nothing. Tomorrow she should think about driving to her parents' home, but for now, the only mandate was to watch nature unfold before her. A boat roared by, disturbing the calm, and when it disappeared around the island in the middle of the lake, the silence descended like a curtain.

"Hayley?"

The deep voice was so close that Hayley jumped and swung around to face the sound.

"David."

"I didn't mean to startle you." His voice matched the soft evening sounds around them.

He stood about three feet away, towering over her, reminding her of their very first meeting. She saw that he was dressed as impeccably as ever in navy corduroy slacks and a short-sleeved pullover that displayed tanned, muscular arms. She regarded him coolly, gratified that she had made progress since she had last seen him. After the first surprise, Hayley's heart behaved quite sensibly.

"How did you find me?" she asked.

He made no attempt to approach, only answered, "Peter told me you left to visit your parents. They said you would be here."

Hayley turned away from him to stare at the lake again, irritation surfacing at Peter and her parents for letting him know her whereabouts.

David walked around to face her and crouched down to meet her eyes. "We need to talk," he said.

"I can't imagine why."

"I was wrong. I'm sorry."

The bluntness of the apology drew Hayley's full attention to the man studying her with such intensity. He looked tired — no, exhausted — but somehow different. Determined, but humble. Hayley acknowledged the apology with a slight nod, and a hint of a grin appeared on David's face.

"At least you're not going to throw me off the property."

Hayley knew that the grin was only a preview of a smile that could be her undoing, and she wasn't ready to let him off easily. She dropped her eyes to the ground and shifted a few pebbles across the grass. She heard his voice beside her, resignation weighing the tone down.

"I didn't expect a warm welcome, but I owed you the apology and an explanation."

She lifted her chin. "On that we agree."

He flinched and looked away for a moment. Then he met her eyes again. "Will you walk with me a little while? I'd like to talk with you about what happened, then I'll leave."

Hayley considered refusing, knowing how persuasive he could be and how vulnerable her heart still was. But he had driven three-and-a-half hours to see her. The least she could do was hear him out. "All right," she said quietly.

David held out his hand. She ignored it and struggled up on her own, shaking her legs to loosen them from sitting on the ground. He shoved his hands in his jeans pockets, and turned toward an opening in the trees where a path broke through.

Hayley stepped in beside him.

"I am sorry," David spoke finally with a low vibrancy that sent shivers through her shoulders. "I accused you of something that you would never have considered."

"What changed your mind?"

A smile tugged at his profile as Hayley looked at him. "You... and events. We won the contract."

"Which you did not expect."

"Not after you started working for Jameson."

Hayley stopped in astonishment. "It's clear that there really isn't anything to talk about." She spun on her heel and strode from him, surprise and anger driving her away.

"Hayley!" In a few strides, he had grabbed her arm and swung her around. At her outraged and pointed look at her arm, he dropped his hand. "Please." Frustration drew his hands back into his pockets, and he shifted on his feet, sweeping the trees and sky with a glance before focusing on Hayley, a plea on his face as well as in his voice. "Just listen. Please. It's the only thing I'll ask of you."

The pain generated by his statement let Hayley know that listening was not the only thing she wanted him to ask of her. She shook herself. All the weeks of separation were falling away just walking with him. She owed him her attention, nothing else.

"All right," she said.

For several minutes, Hayley sensed the uneasiness of the man beside her. The humid evening air and the insistent chirrup of crickets did nothing to dispel the energy surrounding him. He walked with his hands clasped behind his back, his head bowed slightly in thought.

"Finding those papers came at the worst possible time," David said at length. "The night before, I had barely restrained myself from throttling Peter when I saw his arms around you at the restaurant. When I saw the note, I saw you together."

"You were jealous," Hayley murmured.

He nodded. "Blindly so. Then we won the contract. I knew for certain that I had made a disastrous mistake. If you were working for PAJ and you had lent your ideas to their proposal, Mansfield could not have won."

Hayley recognized the compliment. "It *was* a good proposal."

"The best," David stated with a conviction that betrayed his deep pride in the work. "I realized you were right. I have been a coward."

Remembering the accusation, Hayley blushed. "Not in everything," she said quickly.

"But in the most important things. I knew I couldn't live with that. To remedy things, I started with the situation I had fostered. If you hadn't put those papers in that envelope, who did? And why?" He slipped his hands in his pockets and threw her a sheepish look. "I didn't dare ask any of the proposal team. It seems when they heard of your leaving, I became the company pariah. The only person still talking to me without an accusation behind every word was Maggie. To my shock, when I showed her the envelope, she confessed."

Hayley gasped and clasped his arm to stop him. "Maggie?" She shook her head. "But why?"

"The day before I found the envelope, I asked Maggie what she thought about you managing the library operations of the project. I knew you were inexperienced, but the organizing skills you showed during writing and your ideas — well, it was clear that you should have a hand in running the operation." He paused and added, "And I wanted you there."

The thrill of his praise flew through Hayley.

David continued walking, his pace faster as the story unfolded. "I learned that Maggie was furious with me for stepping over her. She thought that she should be the one to handle the project. She had been disappointed when I asked you to write the proposal. Handing you a part in the management was too much to bear."

"What did she hope to gain?" Hayley asked, still surprised by her supervisor's actions.

"She hoped that I would take you off the project. Which is what I meant to do. She never dreamed you would quit."

"I still don't understand how she timed it. How did she know when you would come down to the office?"

He shrugged. "Quite easily. I called and told her the morning you were at the dentist. I was checking to see if you were back yet. Maggie answered, said you weren't expected until after lunch, and I told her I would be down to look for some notes. As you said, your note was among the papers on your desk, and she did the rest."

"Maggie," Hayley murmured. "I can hardly believe it."

"I misread her," David said apologetically. "She never expressed any interest in project work, and she did such a good job in the library." He continued in a rush, "Once I'd talked to Maggie, the full impact of what I had done became clear. I had accused not only you, but Peter. Unjustly. For the second time."

Hayley's heart jolted in astonishment. David was actually referring to the terrible breach between him and his best friend.

"I called your apartment several times, but you were never home, so I decided to call Peter. Of course, he knew you had left town but was determined to make me suffer. I finally offered to buy him a drink so we could talk." David smiled at the thought. "It turned into a lot of drinks and half the night. Peter told me what I had known all along but had been unwilling to accept. Julia was a spoiled child, beautiful and witty, but utterly self-centered. She wanted me because I was headed for a vice-presidency, and she was selfish enough to resent anything or anyone that seemed to keep me off track."

Silence descended between them. The path wound away from the shoreline and back in the direction of the cottage. The light was fading quickly, turning the forest path into a private corridor cut off from the world and impervious to interruption.

"Hayley?"

"Yes?"

"I came to tell you that if you want your job back, it's there."

"What about Maggie?"

"She resigned as soon as I made it clear she couldn't stay at Mansfield."

Disappointment encompassed Hayley's soul. David had come to offer her the job that was rightly hers. There was no mention of anything personal, no hint that he wanted more. Just the job.

"Of course if you prefer working at PAJ," David said quietly, "I'll understand."

"The job at PAJ is temporary until I can get something else," Hayley said and rejoiced at the surprise that flew across David's face.

With an eagerness that Hayley remembered from many proposal sessions, David continued his campaign. "You can write the job description any way you like. Work on the project, manage the library, a little of both. I don't care. I'll stay out of your way as much as I can."

The last statement smacked Hayley sharply. He would still avoid her. The lure of the job was powerful — to have control of part of the project she had designed would be marvelous. But how could she work beside him under his self-imposed exile from her?

"You don't need to tell me now," David continued. "If you'll consider it, I'll call you next week, and you can give me your decision then."

Hayley felt that she could breathe again. "Yes," she said, "I'll consider it."

They had reached the clearing below the cottage again. The spotlight on the corner of the house had lit automatically with the approaching dusk, and it threw a beckoning ring of light onto the dark ground.

Under the light, David held out his hand to Hayley. "Thank you for listening."

In slow motion, Hayley lifted her hand to meet his. She hesitated to touch him. This touch might be the last she would ever have of him. A handshake would seal her to his impersonal demeanor. To endure that would be unbearable.

David surrounded her hand with his. Instead of the expected handshake, his other hand suddenly captured hers, and waves of warmth communicated themselves to her. When she looked into his face, Hayley shuddered at the uncertainty hovering in the lines across his forehead and in his pleading eyes.

He kept her hand in his own and whispered, "Can you ever forgive me?"

Hayley's heart soared. "I already have," she answered.

An inner light flared in David's eyes. His hand reached up to touch Hayley's cheek with such tenderness that the earth under Hayley's feet turned to clouds. "Perhaps it's not too late," he murmured.

"Too late?" Hayley repeated, struggling to maintain her hold on solid ground while David's fingers flowed across her skin.

"Do you realize how much you frighten me? If I open my heart and my life to you, you can wreck my sanity with one harsh word. I forced you out of my company, but when you left, I reached for the phone every day to share some small incident with you, only to remember you were gone." David's hands grasped her shoulders. "I'm afraid you'll hurt me, drag emotions from me I never knew I had. But without you, I'm lost. I'm still afraid, but I'm willing to take the risk. I love you, Hayley. I want you beside me. I need you beside me — in my work and in my life. I want to marry you. Please say we can try again."

The world stopped, then spun wildly for Hayley. With shaking fingers, she traced his forehead and cheek. When her fingers touched his lips, David gently kissed their tips.

"Hayley? Say something."

"Oh, David, I love you, too" was the fervent answer.

In an instant, she was in his arms, his lips searing hers with a promise that the future would be a risk well worth taking.

ABOUT THE AUTHOR

First there were crayon drawings in grade school, then books of space travel, mysteries and espionage. I've always carried stories in my head and written them down. In college, my aunt sent me a box of books, including Kathleen Woodiwiss' *The Flame and the Flower*. I caught romance fever and never looked back. Now with several books and awards to my credit, I continue to write and promote books that lift the Spirit.

When I'm not writing, I enjoy crocheting, bird watching, traveling, and jigsaw puzzles. I'm an avid fan of romance in all its variety, and my favorite diversion is a well-written book with a happy ending. Thank you for reading *A Love He Can Trust*.

Connect With Me Online
On Facebook: facebook.com/lavernestgeorge/
On Twitter: https://twitter.com/LaVerneStGeorge
On Goodreads: LaVerne St. George
My Blog: Writing in the Spirit
My Website: LStGeorge.com
Sign up for my Newsletter: http://oi.vresp.com?fid=38f6c4675a

OTHER BOOKS BY LAVERNE ST. GEORGE

Explore these titles at LaVerne's website (www.LStGeorge.com)

CAROUSEL MAGIC. Pittsburgh Connections, Book 2. Contemporary Sweet Romance Novelette. Available in print and eBook.

Thomas Martin never lets feelings get in the way of doing business. As the new owner of the local amusement park, he's determined to replace the old carousel with video games. The town's mayor, Ginger Fairchild, is equally determined to save the vintage carousel from the bulldozer. Tom's broken childhood left him with a strong sense of reality, but not much experience with fantasy or fun. Ginger is sure that if she can encourage Tom to have a little fun, he'll change his mind about this special ride. The park needs a lot of work before opening day. There's not much time. Can Ginger persuade Tom of the carousel's value before it's too late? Does the carousel have enough magic left to change just two more hearts?

AUTUMN'S KISS. Sweet Romance Novella Anthology from Open Book Romances. Available as eBook.

Looking for more Sweet Romance? Try this novella anthology! Eight sweet stories of love. Eight great authors. Eight ways to celebrate autumn.

Falling in love is timeless. From a sexy medieval stonemason to a big-time businessman — Regency England to Napa Vineyards — this selection of Historical, Contemporary, Paranormal and Time-Travel romance novellas is sure to capture your heart.

THE MASTER'S PLAN. Contemporary Inspirational Romance. Available as eBook from Astraea Press and in print directly from the author.

For Caralyn Masters, an accident leaves lingering effects — she grieves for her sister and automobiles give her the literal shakes. She focuses on her job as a university librarian and on creating a charitable fund to support closed-head trauma research, but money is tight. While hiking in the Ozarks, she shares a trail shelter with a wet and weary hiker. He's charming. She's attracted. Things are looking up.

Jason Montague counts his blessings. His unplanned hike ended in the company of an experienced hiker. He's captivated by Cara, but as the Doncaster Foundation's chairman, he holds the future of her charity in his hands. When he's forced to reveal his epilepsy, his hope for a personal relationship vanishes. Back at Doncaster's Midwest office, Jason discovers missing money, a missing employee, and negative media spin. Things are not looking good.

~Bad Things Happen. Then Love Steps In.

SPECIAL EXCERPT FROM...
THE MASTER'S PLAN

When Cara stepped up the two wide plank steps into the next shadowed hut, this time a jewelers, Jason followed, but only after extracting a promise of another joust. She moved to study the intricate patterns the artist had created from metal.

Her gaze moved over rings and bracelets, then held.

On a background of deep green velvet lay a necklace of delicate silver filigree, the swirls and ropes of metal intertwined to form a collar several inches wide. The workmanship was breathtaking. Cara reached out and took the piece in her hands.

A tiny price tag dangled from a string at the clasp. She read the number and swallowed hard. For a brief moment, she considered pulling her wallet out and handing over her credit card. She wanted this. It was the type of necklace that deserved appreciation, not for its sparkle and cost, but for the love and care that went into forming each fine silver curve. But over a hundred dollars...

"Try it on," the fatherly man in a feathered cap behind the stand urged.

She began to shake her head, then started as the necklace was taken from her and warm hands draped the silver around her neck. Pleasure as potent as the sun's heat rushed through her.

"Here, let me help." Jason's low voice caressed her.

He brushed her hair off the back of her neck and with a touch that sent trickles of heat down her back, fastened the clasp. She looked down at the collar that lay with surprising lightness. The silver shone with an ethereal iridescence against the gray-blue shirt. Even though the shirt was casual, the necklace lent it elegance. Unconsciously she straightened.

Jason came around to face her. Without moving a muscle, his eyes studied the necklace, then her face and hair. His jaw tightened slightly. A slow flush rose into Cara's cheeks then burned steadily over her whole body.

The craftsman's voice drifted into the mist hovering between them. "It looks good on a woman, doesn't it?"

Jason reached out and fingered the pattern of the metal. Cara stood very still.

"It's beautiful" came his hoarse reply.

He leaned slightly toward her as if drawn by some invisible thread. His eyes darkened.

For Cara, the world stopped. She knew that if he kissed her now, she would be pulled into another dimension. She didn't know if she dared to discover what lay there. But ever since the Ozarks, they had been moving toward this moment as surely as the sun rose and set.

55785352R10074

Made in the USA
Columbia, SC
20 April 2019